Melissa Chan has lived in Europe, the United States of America and (briefly) China. After growing up in the Western Australian wheatbelt, she moved to the Eastern seaboard where she works as a lawyer. Her fiction has appeared in *Ita*, *Womanspeak* and other magazines and she is a contributor to the first Spinifex Press anthology, *Angels of Power and other reproductive creations*. She is currently writing a second murder mystery novel, *One Too Many*, also centred around the lesbian film critic and private detective Francesca Miles. Her collection of short stories, *Getting Your Man*, is soon to be published by Spinifex Press.

TOO RICH

MELISSA CHAN

SPINIFEX PRESS
Australia

Spinifex Press Pty Ltd
504 Queensberry Street
North Melbourne Vic. 3051
Australia

First published by Spinifex Press, 1991

Reprinted 1991

Typeset in 10/11.5pt Sabon by Claire Warren, Melbourne
Production by Sylvana Scannapiego, Island Graphics, Melbourne
Made and printed in Australia by The Book Printer, Victoria
The contents of this book have been printed on 100% recycled paper

CIP
Chan, Melissa, 1947–   .
  Too rich.

  ISBN 1 875559 02 7

  I. Chan, Melissa. II. Title.
A823'.3

Note:

All characters and incidents depicted herein are fictional. No
resemblance to any person or persons living or dead is intended
or to be implied.
    The proverbs appearing at the commencement of each chapter
are taken or adapted from Bueno de Mesquita, *Men Are Pigs*, 1928,
Cornstalk Publishing Company, Sydney; and Nina Farewell, *The Unfair
Sex – An Exposé of the Human Male for Young Women of Most Ages*,
1953, Frederick Muller Ltd, London. Every effort has been made to
trace the copyright holders and the publishers would be pleased to
hear from any copyright holder who has not been able to be traced.

I

In which
Danil Gleixner Dies

There is something about the tenderness
of a woman that goes to a man's heart – but
without a woman's strength his life falls in ruins.

IT WAS AN ordinary day. Most weekdays
Danil left for the office shortly after she had set out for the city.
This morning he had been particularly intent on fixing his
bow-tie 'just right' before she left, asking her how it looked,
appreciating what he called her 'good taste'. It was an attribute
he laughed about, on the one hand, in his way, yet found
valuable in his struggle to rise from the ranks of the tradesman
to the social set. As with many men who came 'up from
below', the social circles in which he and she now moved were
important for his business, and for his liking to get ahead.

Returning from town later, the penthouse was silent (like
other days) as she fumbled with the lock, her hands full of
Beryl Jents shopping bags.

Getting the door open at last, she nudged her way in, pushing with her right Louis Feraud-covered shoulder against the
smooth panelling. The shades were down in the main room,
cutting out the early afternoon glare. Half-consciously she
heard the smooth click of the lock as the door shut behind her.

The bedroom lay to the right, down a wide, L-shaped
passage. Walking toward it, she turned to the left, entering the
walk-in dressingroom that housed their clothes. Although

mostly hers, his hung along one side: suit after suit of fine Italian tailoring; shoes and loafers for every occasion; thirty or so silk ties. Even several hats: Danil fancied himself as a man-about-town, and hats were 'in' in the circles in which he – they – moved.

Silently, and concentrating hard on her morning purchases, she pushed the hangers along the rail. Her hands lingered lovingly on the soft deep-green velvet she drew from the sheets of tissue. She held up the dress, gazing admiringly at her tall, strikingly red-headed figure in the mirror against the darkness of the fabric. Perfect! she hummed to herself, pirouetting as if before a television camera. When the world saw her in this, the men would swoon for her glance, the women's faces tighten – oh! almost (but not quite) imperceptibly: in what passed in Sydney for society, the women were clever at dissimulating. But they knew real class when they saw it and (even more) recognised a worthy rival immediately.

The door of the workout room - the private gym Danil had installed in the penthouse - was almost closed. Humming softly to herself she walked toward it, raising her left hand to push against the opaque glass panel. It resisted her touch. She shoved, then glanced down to see whether a towel or some piece of clothing was jamming it.

It was then that she saw the red sharply contrasted against the white pile of the carpet. Lifting her right foot, she noticed that the sole and edges of her shoe were covered in the red smear. She pushed frantically against the door again, her whole body heaving, this time. It stood solid against her. She began to scream.

'Whaddaya reckon, mate? I've made it, or have I made it?' Inspector Barnaby looked across his wide desk at his visitor, effecting what each knew was the language pattern of his past. Growing up as a kid in Mount Druitt in the western suburbs of Sydney, he had the choice of being a'gin the coppers, or joining them. Without any real appetite for what he thought of as point-less rebellion, Joe Barnaby joined them. And did well.

At forty-two, Inspector Barnaby did not have to police his own kind, the kids out at Rooty Hill or Parramatta who were accused of petty thefts of milk-money, or scarpering with handsful of toys moulded in the image of the Teenage Mutant Ninja Turtles – or whatever was the latest craze, or (the worst sorts of offences) burning down the local school and making off with thousands of dollars worth of computer equipment and videos. (At least, he thought, they're getting the funds out there now to buy the stuff for the schools. Okay, so it gets stolen. But the kids get to use it – whether legally or illegally – and the government's so scared of another riot that it keeps replacing the stuff.)

'I'd say – you've made it!' said Francesca Miles seriously. But her twitching lips gave her away, and the two of them collapsed laughing.

'Not bad for a westie,' hawed Joe, slapping the blotter in front of him. 'And I don't know why I'm wasting my time talking with you,' he exclaimed, pointing a shaking finger at Francesca as her shoulders heaved on the other side of the desk.

'Aw, c'mon Joe, wouldn't hold Turramurra against me, would you?' Francesca quizzed. 'Can I be blamed for my parents' errors?'

Francesca Miles had grown up on Sydney's North Shore; salubrious suburbs which vied with older, established Point Piper and Rose Bay, and parts of Woollahra, east of the city centre. She and Joe Barnaby had met when she was at university, doing an arts degree, like most of her friends. Francesca had later changed to law. He had, a few years later (and probably at her persuasion, she thought, now) begun studying for the Diploma of Criminology. She had tied herself up in a masters degree, majoring in criminal law and criminology. Their courses overlapped and, surprising to some, so did their interests in politics (and film).

'Well, Fran, so you're here covering the Sydney Film Festival.'

'Ah, but taking the opportunity to fit in some "commercial" films, as they say in the trade,' she said, with an exaggerated shrug and a wide grin. 'Guess what I've just had the horror to see, wandering down George Street on a Monday afternoon, nothing to do, nowhere to go, at a loose end and ready for a bit of muck?'

He raised his eyebrows, questioning. '*Sleeping with the Enemy*.

3

That just about says it all, doesn't it?' She grimaced. 'You've gotta laugh, or else you'd cry. And you know I don't ordinarily speak in cliché, or just do it for effect. And boy, is it a time to be affected. Beautiful girl marries handsome man, and what happens? He turns into a monster, keeping her locked up at home apart from the times he'll let her out. So long as she's in *his* company, she can go where she wants – he says. And when she makes a move of her own, well, he just clocks her one. Swiftly. Pounding to the head. Jabbing to the jaw. So long as it doesn't show, he'll do it. Pity is, Joe, that the story's all too true. Could've been a great opportunity to get across the message, sink it home, begin working toward change. Why, thousands of people are going to the film. It's packing 'em in. Yesterday, theatre crowded with women, men, teenagers, kids. . .'

Francesca Miles slapped the note book she was holding on the desk, emphasising her words. 'So here I am, dedicated to the women's cause, looking at a film that could've been good – and confronted with a mishmash that I can say little or nothing good about. Still, at least it was about bashing in the so-called upper echelons. A change from the notion that it's only the wives of the down-and-outs who get the blows.'

She was silent for a moment, recalling the times that Luana had told her of, when her mother had cowered in a corner while her husband, Luana's father, towered above her, shouting and screaming his abuse as he thrashed her with a riding crop. The nights Luana had woken, shivering, in bed next to her, and clung to her in the aftermath of a remembered childhood nightmare, sobbing and crying. Luana – Francesca had met her at Red Ruby's, the lesbian bar in Surry Hills. Soon after, they had left Sydney for Melbourne and a quiet life. An escape for Luana from a world where her father held power in that select group of business magnates who pushed their way through the stock exchange, selling here, buying there, adding nothing to the value of the economy, and less to the lives and well-being of others. East Melbourne might be seen as smug and unexciting, but she and Luana liked it. At least, no Gordon Burton Adams and his conglomerate of companies to intrude so often into their lives. If they avoided the business pages of the *Age*, and the *Fin. Review* altogether, they could pretend – until those nightmares returned – that he no longer existed.

4

Francesca shivered. Straightening her back, she returned to the present, to Joe Barnaby's office in College Street. He leant across the desk, his eyes fixed firmly on hers, a smile playing at his mouth which belied the harshness of his words. 'So, Fran, you're still playing at being a trendy film critic. When're you going to get a *real* job?' Francesca aimed a gentle swipe vaguely in his direction, ready to retort.

The soft but insistent burr of the telephone at Joe Barnaby's hand interrupted. 'Yes?' Joe's voice butted into the mouthpiece. An indecipherable squawking commenced. Francesca saw Joe's eyebrows rise, his face melting into a blank, official pose almost in the same instant.

Just as suddenly as it had begun, the voice stopped. Inspector Barnaby replaced the handset in its cradle and grabbed for his holster which lay on the desk near his right hand. 'Well, kid, this is it,' he grimaced. 'My big chance. Make it – I'm a hero. Fail – I'm dead meat.' He shoved his chair backwards, hoisting himself rapidly into standing position. 'You won't believe this – and I'm not giving anything away; it'll be all over the news and there're television cameras there already. It's Gleixner, Danil Gleixner. Dead. Shot. Looks like suicide – but – there's some question. Hence – Inspector Barnaby at-your-service.'

In mid-stride to the door she stopped him. 'Hey, Barnaby, what about me! Here I am, on the spot, and you're running off without me. Where's that camaraderie you're so hot about. The recognition of women's detection ability and dedication to the job. Just plain old equal rights.'

She was almost spluttering, and angry at herself for her sense of speechlessness. He couldn't get away with it. Okay, she wasn't a member of the force. But she'd known him for years. Even helped (oh, goddess! what was she saying?) – *solved* several of the murders that had led to his taking over as Head of Homicide. And here he was acting as if she didn't exist. Well – almost. Told her who – but not how, not where – and not that she could come too.

He hesitated. Thought rapidly, recalling her swift intelligence when it seemed a killing was unsolvable. It could be seen as unorthodox – taking a private detective on a police job. But – she could (would, he acknowledged, remembering to be fair –

5

and sensible in the light of his need to solve whatever it was about this one that needed to be solved) be useful.

'Okay, Fran. Just this once. But keep quiet when the journos are around. If they catch you out – we could both be gone.'

'Oh sure, sure, Joe. I'll be good.' She looked at him quizzically. 'I'll sink right back into the wallpaper. Or the woodwork. Whatever the accoutrements are at the scene of the death.'

'Apartment. Penthouse. Double Bay. Skye. Right there on the harbour. Live-in girlfriend found him.'

They were walking together to the car, parked on College Street, nose pointing toward the city and the cathedral.

'Well, then, you know no one's likely to pay much attention to me,' laughed Francesca, shrugging her shoulders in a slight moue. 'All eyes on Ms Prince. Ms Elizabeth Prince, isn't it? Twenty to twenty-five years younger than he. Tall, redhead, university graduate. Fine arts, wasn't it? Started out in medicine – but somehow didn't make it. Gleixner met her at the races. Tossed over the earlier model, Rosa, after going to and fro for five years or so. Divorce on the cards?'

Barnaby wove his way through the heavy traffic as he drove up William Street, under the Kings Cross overpass, with the afternoon breeze blowing in the car windows.

'Well, that's the rumour. But I never would've believed he'd really do it. Divorce Rosa, I mean. She's what they call a strong woman. If the truth be known, she probably held the business together. Elizabeth Prince – different type altogether. There was a strong resemblance. Looked like Rosa about fifteen years younger. But had none of the stamina. One for an easy life. That wasn't what Rosa had. She had worked with Danil Gleixner from the day they got together. Same background. Came out here, escaping totalitarianism, from Panama. Setting up here without a penny to their name. Working together in a luxury car-import business. Then the children came along. She kept the books, he travelled around doing sales and the mechanical repair jobs. They built the business together. And then Gleixner apparently wasn't satisfied. Wanted the brains and the toughness of Rosa. And went soft on Prince.'

Joe Barnaby was concentrating hard on the road and the cars banking up behind and ahead of him. But his mind was already churning over what he knew. Sifting through the rumour and

reality known to the police about the media-hungry businessman from somewhere in South America. Arrived here on a
cheap passage, ten dollars in his pocket. Built himself into the
paradigm of a self-made man. Made on the millions produced
by the work of so many others as well as himself. Made out of
his fellow immigrants. Low wages. Fought against unionism.
Got away with below award wages when he could. Yet – despite
it all, a hero to those same men he screwed daily. They saw that
because he had become rich and powerful, albeit from exploit-
ing them, they might make it too. The proverbial pot of gold at
the end of the rainbow lured them into tolerating his authoritarian ways. They wanted to preserve the system the way it was,
so they could (when the miracle happened, they won the lottery,
got lucky, or whatever it was that started the ordinary man on
the road to becoming the head of his own mining corporation, or
supermarket chain, or brewing fortune. . .) use it like he did.
Like he had.

But then – October 1987. The bottom fell out of the share
market. Rumours had it that it was 1929 all over again. Was
Danil Gleixner caught up in it? Overextended? Overcapitalised?
Had he struggled on, wearing the losses, without letting the
general public or the business world know how badly the drop
in the market affected him? Attempted to work on, riding out
the recession that followed. Then found it was too much, that
recovery wasn't 'just around the corner'. That the hoped-for
appearance of the J-curve failed to eventuate. Then – decided it
was better to end it at the end of a gun than suffer the ignominy
of his empire crashing around him, acknowledging that the self-
made man had his feet in the sand, his head in the mud with
the rest of 'em?

'Okay, Constable, I've got it.' Inspector Barnaby and Francesca
Miles stood, their feet planted firmly in the lush pile of the carpet covering the entrance hall of the Skye penthouse that still
held the rapidly cooling body of Danil Gleixner. Elizabeth Prince
had been ferried off, heavily sedated, to a private hospital at
Point Piper, with a police officer set on guard outside her room,
just in case.

'She left here at about 9.00 a.m. to shop and meet a friend,
Suzanne Pleasamore, at David Jones in the city. Took her own

car. Parked at Eixn Industries' private parking area in York Street. Made her way on foot through Grace Brothers and Centrepoint, browsed around in the first- and second-floor boutique clothing areas in David Jones, then went up by elevator to the top floor restaurant. There she met the friend at 10.30 a.m. and they talked until 12.30 p.m., drinking black coffee.'

Joe Barnaby paused, grimacing at Constable Crawshaw who stood ramrod straight before him, his face impassive. 'What the hell do these women talk about, then, old chap?' he said, not expecting an answer. He sensed a slight movement by his side, but Francesca Miles, remembering she was here masquerading as a plain-clothes cop, restrained the sharp retort that leapt to her tongue.

'Any witnesses?'

'The maid saw her go. Serviced apartments, Inspector, and the maid does six of them on this side. She usually leaves Gleixner's 'til last, because they generally leave from between 9.30 a.m. to 10.30 a.m. and return late. The others go earlier and return earlier.'

Constable Crawshaw glanced at his notepad. 'Maid received a call at about 10.30 a.m. saying her sister had been in an accident and that she was wanted immediately at North Shore Hospital. So she didn't actually do the Gleixner penthouse at all today.'

'And the sister?' Francesca broke in, her suspicion of coincidence intruding on her resolution to keep silent whilst the constable completed his report.

Constable Crawshaw looked at her, then at his superior, nodding. 'Yes, it seems to have been a hoax. Sister's fine. Never better. Hadn't been in a car that day or the night before. When the maid got to Royal North Shore no one knew what she was talking about. Didn't have a Nurse Johnson there – the one who was supposed to have made the call. No Nurse Johnson on duty. There was a Nurse Johnson working there, but she left about a month ago.'

The men from forensics had gone, taking with them fingerprint samples and, it seemed, samples of whatever fibres and other particles existed in the penthouse. (And yes, Francesca had noted the absence of any female scientists and recorded it as an area for lobbying Barnaby sometime. Affirmative action in the forensic science laboratory? Why not. After all, most women who did science ended up peering down a microscope, in between having babies and looking after husbands. They could well develop their skills in the police laboratories – and recover the reputation of women in the field after the disaster of the Alice Lynne Chamberlain-'dingo baby' affair and the destruction of slides alleged to be carrying fatal – or exoneratory – evidence.)

She was leaning against the doorframe, gazing down at Barnaby as he knelt scrutinising the floor where Danil Gleixner had lain.

'He shot himself – if he did (and it looks like it at this stage) – with his back to the door. The bullet lodged in his brain, and he slid down jamming the door so that whoever came in couldn't get it open.'

'Thoughtful chap,' said Francesca, an unusually sour sounding in her voice. 'Protecting the women in his life as always – from life (or death). Whatever way you want to look at it. Didn't want them to have to see him stretched out. Spoil their pleasant memories of him. Not his fault the old man had so much blood in him. Got it on her shoes.'

Barnaby looked up. 'Yet he didn't close the door completely before he did it. Fell against it so it closed to, but the tongue didn't go right into the socket. Think of any explanation for that, Fran?'

She shook her head, then wandered into the bedroom, gazing at the opulence with veiled distaste: the ubiquitous lush white carpet; kingsize bed covered in white, six plump, white-covered pillows piled high at the head; one wall gaudily mirrored from ceiling to floor; deep green velvet drapes edging filmy white curtains across wide french windows opening (when they did) on to a terrace overlooking the harbour. (The drapes were obviously chosen to be set off against the titian locks of the lady-of-the-penthouse.)

Turning, Francesca Miles allowed her eyes to stray over the room. It was usually in the intimacy of those closed-off regions of the homes around the nation that the worst crimes were committed. Blows against wives. Acts of violence women too often translated into 'just what a wife has to put up with', when it occurred in the marital bed rather than a back alley. Intrusions into the private worlds of little girls (and some boys) in the guise of 'teaching you to be a grown-up'. Did any clue lie here to the death of Danil Gleixner, one of the richest men in Australia?

Change that to 'people', she thought wryly. If he's one of the richest men, there're no rich women to challenge the title. Except, maybe, now – his wife. Depending on how the will arranges things, she said to herself.

Glancing down, she noticed the scales. 'You can never be too thin, or too rich.' Duchess of Windsor, wasn't it, who said that? Otherwise known as Wallis Simpson. No wonder the British establishment didn't want her as their queen. The thought of having to genuflect to someone who in real life was Mrs *Simpson* was too terrible to have to endure. They chose not to. And she became the Duchess of Windsor, exiled to a life of riches and nothing to do for it, in France and Barbados. Hobnobbing with Hitler. Bartering with the Brownshirts. And leaping on scales at the drop of a hat just to check that all that high living didn't put on a single pound and, hopefully, took several off daily.

'Are you over or under?' Joe Barnaby stood in the doorway. Her face turned red as she turned to him, almost overbalancing and falling from the scales. 'Just checking,' she said. 'I saw the scales here and thought I'd. . .'

'Yes, I know you women,' laughed Barnaby, shaking his finger at her. 'All the same. Jill'd do it too – soon as see a scale, jump on it. Got to know the worst – or the best. If it's under what hers say, then she believes the weight. If it's over, she disregards it. Says it must be wrong. Scales not properly balanced.'

'Well,' said Francesca laughing guiltily. 'That's just what I was thinking. They've got me three pounds overweight – so they must be wrong. Maybe – maybe Elizabeth Prince is so obsessed she keeps them over so as not to delude herself into thinking she weighs less than she does.'

'Hey, now. Where're your feminist principles, Fran?' said Barnaby. 'It could've been Gleixner, you know. I've got to confess we men are really just as bad. Oh, hide it from everyone, that's true. But we're probably just as obsessed about weight as women are, if the world only knew it. Maybe he leapt out of bed each morning and on to the scales before he did his work out in the gym.'

It was a well-laid-out gymnasium in the large room neighbouring the dressingroom. Exercise bicycle. Running ramp. Weight-lifting equipment. Medically adjusted scales for the aficionado, with weights attached to a long arm which rested at waist level, to be adjusted according to the bulk of the person standing on the slightly raised platform. Mini-trampoline. You name it. Gleixner had it.

'Well, what d'you reckon, Joe? Murder or suicide?' Francesca stepped down from the scales, looking at Barnaby questioningly.

'One thing we do know, Fran. Whoever pointed the gun – whether it was the man himself or some ill wisher – knew what they were doing and intended to do it. It was no accident. And, likewise, it sure as hell ain't manslaughter!'

II

In which Rosa Gleixner has her Say

*Men are like honey bees, flying from one flower
to another and taking nectar from each.*

'WHAT THE HELL do you think you're doing in my apartment?' Startled, Joe Barnaby and Francesca Miles looked from each other to the large, hennaed brunette who stood, arms akimbo, in the wide open doorway. 'Get out, and take your bloody notebooks and nosiness with you.' She motioned at them with a thrusting finger.

'Mrs Gleixner, M'am, Inspector Barnaby and this is—'

Before Barnaby could finish, Rosa Gleixner (for it was she) clattered into the room, her spiked heels pounding against the highly polished parquet floor in the entrance way. 'I said, get out. Get out. Get out. Get out.' With hardly a pause, she moved over to the mantel above the open fireplace and with one long arm swept on to the floor a large cutglass vase of red poppies that had been standing there. It landed with a sharp, splintering sound. Water splashed on to carpet and hearth. The poppies fell like splotches of blood against the white pile. 'And now, you can go.'

It was like a final command from someone who was used to having her way. But it had no effect on Joe Barnaby, who motioned to Rosa that she should be seated on the couch he had recently vacated.

'This is *my* property,' she repeated. 'You sit—' she poked at

Francesca, 'and you stand—' she prodded at Barnaby, 'on *my* chair and *my* floor. With *him* dead – Danil gone—' She threw her hands up above her head, gesturing heavenwards. 'It belongs to me. It is mine, mine, mine.' At the last 'mine' she burst into a loud wailing, sobs coming from deep down. Suddenly, she flung herself upon the couch, her fingers clutching at her hair, her face buried in the white leather.

'No, I was nowhere near the place this morning.' Rosa Gleixner had recovered her poise, the recovery largely consisting of ceasing to moan and wail, then plunging into the depths of a huge red handbag to find a comb, deep cerise lipstick, and solid gold compact. After dabbing at her eyes, then applying powder and rouge to her cheeks, and stabbing somewhat wildly at her lips with the Helena Rubinstein colour, Passionflower, that protruded, after a savage twisting, from the lipstick capsule, she had sat, patiently, waiting for the questions she knew would come.

'I arrived back in Sydney only today, this morning. Flew in from Hong Kong, and went straight to the house in Rose Bay.'

She shut her lips firmly, looking at Inspector Barnaby as if to defy him to prove her wrong.

'Mrs Gleixner, the sooner we get through this questioning, the sooner we – the police – can get out of your life. The lives of all of you – all of the Gleixner family,' he said, kicking himself mentally for his stupidity when that gave rise to another stream of invective, which he ought to have predicted.

'Yes, but what about her. That – that – *girl* friend. The tart he had around. D'you mean to say you're not questioning her? Leaving her out of it? Just getting stuck into me and my family?'

She threw a poisonous glance at Francesca. 'The two of you – don't you know that he'd never kill himself. *Never*. Danil was just not like that. Always thinking that whatever was happening now, however good it was, the best was around the corner. Just waiting for him. No, he's got to have been killed. And – and it's *that* woman. The sooner you get moving and question *her* – arrest her – the sooner we can get back to living. . .living without him.'

Hurriedly Inspector Barnaby put the next question, hoping to divert her from the sobs which threatened to break out again.

'Hong Kong. You were there on business, Mrs Gleixner?' He raised his eyebrows in enquiry.

True to the media accounts of 'Sunny' Gleixner's daily travels, Rosa Gleixner confirmed that for her, business meant partying and parties meant business. 'It was a post-wedding wind-down. Just a little get together for myself and Lady Merthers, with Suzy Williams and Trudy Shoeburne flying up from Sydney and the Gold Coast to meet us there. And the Duchess Aziza and her daughter Alyssia flying in from Rome. All on my gold card, of course.'

Francesca looked at Joe Barnaby with barely hidden distaste. A sole parent having to survive, with two children, on eight thousand dollars or so a year in 'the lucky country' Australia, and this – this – she hardly wanted to give Rosa Gleixner the status that her sex would ordinarily grant her in Francesca Miles' ideology – throwing thousands around just for a jaunt out of the country for the weekend. 'And you were there for – how long, Mrs Gleixner?' asked Francesca, her voice low and controlled.

'Oh – two, three days. Let me see – the wedding went off on Sunday. Last Sunday week.' Sunny Gleixner paused, thinking back on the glorious weeks leading up to the marriage of her younger daughter, Mirna, to Charles, the eldest son of the Tysons, one of the wealthiest families in Western Australia. And one of the oldest. Best bred. Large tracts of land running from Albany to Esperance. Great-great-greats coming out with the first colonists to the Swan River Settlement. Old family home on the original land granted by Governor Stirling. A second home at Peppermint Grove, gardens sweeping down through an olive grove to the Swan River foreshore. Aah! Those weeks had been worth living for. . .

She was dragged back to the present by the intensity of Francesca Miles' eyes gazing at her insistently, waiting for a complete answer.

'Well – it took us three days to get over the wedding breakfast. If I'm honest, after they'd gone, Mirna looking so sweet in her pale pink suit, and Charles – Charles so tall and handsome, whatever he wears— Well, they went off to honeymoon at Yanchep, down the coast. Such a sunny place, Yanchep. Just right for young honeymooners. And they're off to Europe later on in the year, of course. When Charles can get away from the sheep and the wheat – business, you know.'

She made a visibly conscious effort to recall the question she was answering, and it came out in a rush. 'Three – call it four days in Hong Kong.'

'So – you left Perth and arrived when, Mrs Gleixner?' Francesca's voice was firm and compelling. Mrs Gleixner answered at once. 'The flight left Thursday night – late. Arrived Hong Kong the next day. We two – Lady Merthers and I – flew up together, and met the others at the hotel. The Duchess and Alyssia arrived the day before. Couldn't make the wedding, unfortunately. A death in the family, you know. They take such things so seriously in Europe. But they had to have a break from the pressure of continual mourning, and took the days in Hong Kong. We cheered them up.'

'And – you stayed—?' It was Francesca again, getting facts – dates, times, places, people – straight in her own head. Wanting to be sure that if there were anything here that bore further investigation, she would get a sense of what it was as soon as she could from at least one of the major witnesses – major players, she corrected herself. Everyone – yes, everyone – was a suspect until proven otherwise by elimination – or because there was no unlawful killing.

'The Friday, over to the Monday. Trudy Shoeburne and Lady Merthers left earlier, to fly back to Perth. We others arrived back this morning – 9.35 a.m.'

She looked at Joe Barnaby and Francesca Miles with an expression mixed of gloating, triumph, horror and despair. 'And here I am – no sooner do I arrive at Rose Bay than I hear it on the news. It's Danil. Danil who was always so alive and wonderful – well, until she – she got her claws into him. Danil dead. Dead.'

She sighed, clutching her right hand to her rather large bosom.

Probably attempting to signify her heart, thought Francesca. If she has one. Then she caught herself in the midst of such an obvious display of lack of charity, and fixed a more sympathetic expression on her features. She *had* to sympathise. After all, this was one of the sisters – well, not quite. But no woman was irredeemable. Unconvertible. Unable to realise the error of her ways, unable to correct the sins of a past, frivolous life. Greater surprises of conversion to a real concern for women, a desire to change the world, had occurred. There was no reason why Rosa Gleixner should not be susceptible to consciousness raising. She had, of course, turned her back in a serious way on her fellow women. Wasting time, money, media space in the triviality of her jet-setting life (or the jet-setting life to which she aspired) which could better have been used on the pressing issues of the day – childcare, criminal assault at home, rape, sexual harassment, equal pay. But – all things were possible. Why, the death of Danil Gleixner and the need to seriously consider the running of the various businesses in his name could be the necessary impetus. If she were left in control of Eixn Enterprises, of course . . . Breaking into her thoughts, Joe Barnaby took over again.

'Mrs Gleixner, I'll have my sergeant make a written record of your movements, that you can check over to make sure we've got it right. But may we fill in some background, so that we've got the picture,' he paused, but it wasn't a question. Inspector Barnaby's style was to be polite – oh, yes, so polite – but to get the information he wanted, anyway. Just assume they'd go along with you, and most of them would. A technique he'd learned when he first joined the force. No need for bright lights, isolation rooms and telephone books. Not for Inspector Barnaby of the CIB, anyway. Never had been his approach. And it paid off. If you were straightforward with people, generally they were straightforward with you. He went on. 'Mrs Gleixner I understand that you spent a lot of your time at Rose Bay, and a lot of time out of the country. Do you know a lot about your – your former husband's business affairs?'

'Business affairs? Business affairs?' she replied, a withering tone in her voice, which adopted an American idiom in her agitation. 'Look, you'd better believe I know a lot about "his" business affairs. It was *our* business, after all. We built it up together, from scratch. He always used to say he landed here with ten dollars in his pocket. Well, let me tell you five dollars of that ten dollars was mine. And he was happy enough in those early years, with me, with us working together to build a new life. My god! It was a good life, too.'

She glared at Joe and Francesca, almost threatening them to deny the truth of what she said. They maintained a discrete silence, willing her to continue, knowing that the only way they would understand what had happened at the Skye Apartments that morning was by listening not only to her words, but to what lay behind them.

'A passionate man, he was. Passionate and hard working. Oh, you couldn't fault my Danil. Not then. Not for the first five years, anyway, give or take a few months. But then Daniella was born. And he thought the sun shone out of her eyes. She became the subject of his passion. Oh – nothing a father shouldn't do, of course. Just that the business, the work, his life – he began to live it for her, not for me.'

Rosa Gleixner's eyes clouded over again. But this time it was not with tears. It was a film of remembering, recalling for her interrogators the past years and the birth of their eldest child. Followed by Tomas, the only son. A disappointment to a father who adhered, still, to medieval notions of 'eldest born', and devoted the major part of his time and attention away from the business to his daughter Daniella. Daniella Ruby Gleixner. Named for him, and for his mother, who had died back home in Bolivia, when he was five years old. But he retained a photograph of her, one of those old, browning, sepia-toned cardboard-backed, posed portraits: 'Daniella grows more like her every day,' he would say, taking the photo from its special pocket in this wallet, and holding it up to her face.

Oh, the passion between them came back at odd intervals. But as he became more and more immersed in the business, developing the import-export business into a multinational company, then trading shares and, much later, horses the passion cooled. All the while he depended on her, Rosa, to keep the books, take the phone calls then, later on, hostess the dinner parties he saw as indispensable to making his way into the world of business and – as she feared it – sharp deals.

Ten years after the birth of Daniella, eight years after the birth of Tomas, the passion returned for a short time, resulting in the baby of the family, Mirna. Mirna Joy. Ironic, really. For it was then, not long afterward, that she knew he was expending his energies not only in the business, and his passion not only in encouraging Daniella in her wilful, spoilt-child ways. No, then began the affairs. Short term, certainly, but painful for her nonetheless. Who wanted to believe she was an old shoe, ready to be thrown off at any convenience? What woman wanted to accept her husband was a philanderer, delighting younger women with his smooth charm? Especially when that smooth charm continued, against her better judgement, to charm her.

Still, she knew always that she was special to him, the principal one, the one he would always come running back to. Did always come running back to. Until – until Elizabeth Prince came along.

She could hardly speak her name. Could hardly think it. Elizabeth Prince. Oh, yes, it took her a while, Rosa (Sunny as the media, too, had now come to call her, when she popped up as a regular fixture in the social pages of more and more afternoon and Sunday newspapers), to realise that this one was different. With this one, if she, Rosa, wanted to keep Danil then she, Rosa, would have to work hard at it.

And work hard, she did. For five years. Or, maybe, just over five years. Attending at the health studio in Double Bay four times – sometimes five times – a week. Visiting Madam Fuchi's beauty salon in the Village most mornings for a facial; every week for hair treatments; every second week for leg and underarm waxing. Had the upper-inside parts of her thighs, and groin, waxed too, to denude them of the pubic hair that knotted itself between her legs. There was little she didn't do to remain young. Or to try to retain her once youthful looks. But childbearing and the hard work of the early years had thickened her waist and upper legs. Her bosom sagged. She began to contemplate surgical nipping and tucking. Liposuction was all the rage in Melbourne. Maybe she should go down for a couple of weeks. Say she needed a rest. Get the cellulite that the beauty salon always found at the tops of her legs removed. Return a new woman!

But then there were reports of negligence actions against the doctor specialising in the practice. Legs ruined rather than rejuvenated. Slashing scars rather than smooth skin. She decided not to go. Just at the time that Danil decided *he* would. Go, that was.

He went. Elizabeth Prince had been set up in the plush penthouse at Skye, the flashest apartment building in Sydney. Built by one of the now burgeoning construction companies, and new money. Five years after the affair had begun, and he had spent his life running back and forth between the two of them, all the while expanding the business, buying race horses and running them at the Perth and Melbourne Cup, at Caulfield and on the Pacific circuit, plunging money into deals, taking on massive government and private projects. Most of the buildings in the city centre housed some arm of Eixn Enterprises. The massive hotel, shopping and convention centre just begun in Martin Place was topped already by a massive Eixn 'Import-Export' sign. He had a way with getting contracts over other tenders, some from overseas. And he left her. For thirty-three-year-old Elizabeth Prince.

'I hate her. It should have been her, not him.' Rosa Gleixner spoke with a passion of her own. 'What right did she have, coming into a happy family and breaking it up. What right did she have, to deprive my children of their father? No child should have to learn that her father – his father – is smitten with someone of – of – such little – relevance.'

She was struggling for words to describe her opinion of the woman who had come between her and Danil Gleixner.

Or was it, more seriously, the coming between her and Eixn Import-Export Enterprises that concerned Rosa Sunny Gleixner, wondered Francesca Miles and Joe Barnaby simultaneously. They had to get a look at the will, and learn more about the current financial standing of Eixn Enterprises. Why, after all, would the man shoot himself when it seemed he had (as they said in the proverbs) everything to live for: company expanding, race horses running, balance of payments favourable - to him, industrial unrest contained (on his wharves), old-model wife traded in for new? Why? Or, perhaps more accurately, *would* he?

III

In which Rosa Gleixner's Parents Support their Daughter

*A man who is willing to spend his time
and money freely in order to win a woman
may be the most lovable kind of male –
but beware when it is not his money.*

THE STREET LIGHTS were on, and Kings Cross was thronging with its usual complement of tourists, lairs, prostitutes, and squalor as Francesca Miles and Joe Barnaby made their way back to the city and police headquarters in College Street. They had finally left the Skye Apartments, Rosa Gleixner and the once-more immaculate gymnasium with its fancy equipment, shower and obligatory spa. But not before her lawyer came striding in to the scene, telling Rosa to keep her counsel with him before answering any more questions.

'My client is perfectly happy to co-operate, Inspector,' said Grant Webster smoothly, moving protectively to Rosa's side. 'But she's had a terrible shock and I'm taking her home to Rose Bay. Here's my card. Telephone me tomorrow and we'll be able to arrange a suitable time for you to speak with her.'

Rosa Gleixner had different ideas. Holding her tongue was not her idea of co-operating, and she burst out before counsel could be taken. 'Grant, tell them to get out of my penthouse.

I've told them all they want to know. And now I want to stretch out on my bed, in front of my television set, with no one to disturb me until I'm good and ready. And that means the media, too.'

Recovered, now, from the tears that had intermittently threatened to interrupt her monologue on life with Danil Gleixner, life without Danil Gleixner, and life after Danil Gleixner, Sunny was once more in control.

'Yes, Rosa,' said Grant Webster solicitously. (She had been rich before, he thought, and now she was way and above his richest client. And he didn't intend to lose her by putting a foot wrong.)

'Well, you heard the lady. I'm sure you don't want me to have to call the Commissioner, do you? Never good for the career to have too many complaints, especially not at the very top, is it?'

He smiled, making a motion toward the telephone, the handpiece of which had long since been removed from its cradle to silence the continual ringing.

The media lay in wait outside, well served by car phones, mobile phones and (for the less well-resourced) the telephone box on the corner. (It was working, as a number of news reporters had discovered.) Adhering strongly to the dictate of their trade, these journalists had a persistence which had to be silenced at the source. At least, thought Francesca, until it was useful to make use of their insights. Often wrong, that's true, through paying too much attention to rumour. But equally often their recitation of what they thought to be the facts (together with their speculation as to motive and events) was likely to trigger off in her some plan of action. Thus they led her closer to a solution to whatever puzzle it was confronting her – or, for that matter, the police.

Grant Webster had obviously not had much experience with reporters, despite handling Rosa Gleixner's legal affairs. Too quickly, he lifted the handpiece and replaced it. Instantly, it rang. 'Yes?' he barked into the telephone. 'No. No she's not able to speak with you. No. No she won't be coming out for the cameras. Yes. The police are still here. But they're on their way out.' With a sharp goodbye he slammed down the phone. Immediately it rang again. He picked it up. 'Hello.'

The others could hear the voice on the other end asking to

speak with Sunny Gleixner. 'She's not speaking with anyone,' said Grant Webster, running his left hand over a now glistening forehead. 'No, you can be as persistent as you like. She'll speak with you when she's good and ready. And she's neither. And don't ring again.'

Inspector Barnaby moved gently over to Webster's side, and pressed down on the cradle sharply, then lifted his hand to take the hand piece. 'Leave it off the hook unless you want to be doing that all night,' he said. 'We'll be on our way. But— ' he turned to Rosa Gleixner. 'Don't leave town. No trips to Hong Kong or Paris. Not for the next few days, anyway. We've still got some checking to do, and we'll be setting the same requirement on everyone else closely associated with Mr Gleixner.'

Turning to Grant Webster, who was leaning against the mantel shelf and gazing pensively around the room, he asked. 'Do you know who was Danil Gleixner's lawyer? We'll have to be in touch with them to sift through some of the background to this – this – all this. And we'd like the addresses of close family. Have to check them all out. The sooner the better.'

'Merthers, Dixon, Sandridge and Sampson,' said Webster automatically. 'They're in the AMP Building down by the Quay. Twenty-seventh floor. As for family – Mirna's probably still at Yanchep. But you could try the Tyson residences – Esperance or Peppermint Grove. If you really want to interrupt the poor girl in the middle of her honeymoon. As for Tomas. Goes under the name of Tom Eixn, now. And your guess is as good as mine. And Daniella. . . Well, she's taken up with – whadda they call it – the Women's Libbers – Women's Movement. Involved in some campaign for a women's refuge on the North Shore. Some new idea that services are lacking amongst the affluent few, it seems.'

He grimaced. 'Got some plan for revolutionising the middle-classes or something. At least, that's what she's said whenever I've tried to talk sense into her. What a waste. Especially with Danil wanting her to take over the business from him. . .'

He stopped, realising he was forgetting his own warning to Rosa to clam up until the setting was in her favour, and she could control what she said and what she didn't say, as well as the direction of the questions. Shrugging his shoulders he turned to her. 'Well, Rosa, what d'you say about a short drink? There must be some brandy about. Good for shock. Its medicinal qualities far outweigh any of those pills the doctors dole out.'

Looking back at Inspector Barnaby, he nodded. 'Goodbye, then. We'll expect a call early afternoon tomorrow. I think Mrs Gleixner will be prepared to answer your questions then. But until then – it's goodbye and shut the door gently as you go.'

He inclined his head vaguely in Francesca's direction, making it clear that, for him, any discussion was now closed.

Taking their leave, Francesca Miles and Joe Barnaby moved toward the door. They had done all they wanted to do for one afternoon and evening. And it didn't hurt, sometimes, to allow an authoritarian type to believe he had one up on the police – or a private detective, if only he knew that was what she was, Francesca thought. Turning suddenly at the door, Barnaby motioned toward the end of the apartment housing master-bedroom and gymnasium. 'You can use them now. We've done everything we want to. For the time being, at least. And it's all clear.'

In a gentler voice he spoke to Mrs Gleixner, 'I'm not able to say when we'll be releasing the body for burial. We'll let you know as soon as possible, but these things take time. There's no way we can fix a date on it, but we recognise the difficulties confronting the family in circumstances such as this, and I can only assure you we'll keep that in mind and act as expeditiously as possible.'

He nodded to the two of them, as they stood closely, side-by-side, in front of the open fireplace. Raising her hand in a slight wave, Francesca Miles bid her goodbyes, too.

They left – only to fight their way through the seething mob, pushing microphones and television lenses towards them, at the front entrance. 'Goddess, sometimes I wonder is it worth it?' shouted Francesca over the noise. 'Impossible to hear any of your questions, or anyone else's, much less answer them,' she muttered to the nearest journalist, a woman who was grabbing at her with one hand and thrusting the microphone under her mouth with the other.

Hands joined, Inspector Barnaby and Francesca Miles pushed their way out, Inspector Barnaby giving an 'on the run' comment, 'Yes, it's Mr Danil Gleixner who was shot. There appear to be no suspicious circumstances at this stage, but we've got a job to do, and we're doing it. There'll be a press conference at police headquarters tomorrow, at 10.00 a.m. sharp to go over the details for release to you all. Until then – no further comment. You've got enough. That's it. There ain't no more.'

Waving in a slight salute, Joe Barnaby kept going, towards his car at the kerb. Head down, Francesca led the way.

'Well, whaddaya reckon, Fran? Suicide? Murder? Misadventure? Changed your mind since we last spoke?' Francesca stretched out in the passenger seat, relaxed in the comfort of familiarity. She and Joe had known each other since – well, since they met up on different sides of the barriers during the Viet Nam War protest days. Joe Barnaby, Constable Barnaby it was, then, staring at her with scared eyes. Afraid that she'd grab his balls or something, Francesca thought now, grinning slightly. But she hadn't. And he hadn't arrested her, either, as she had been afraid he would. Oh, she'd been arrested before. And at later demonstrations. But this was a particularly vicious occasion, police dragging women by the hair along the footpath, grabbing at their breasts as they manhandled them into the paddy wagons. Francesca wasn't scared of standing by her demonstrating mates. But her head was throbbing from a bang it had received from another cop's nightstick, and she didn't feel up to more, just at that time. They'd wandered off together, through the crowd. Now she thought about it, she guessed that Joe'd been risking his job: leaving his post; deserting his colleagues. Well, it hadn't been desertion, really. Just a breather down by the stairs leading into that restaurant – what had it been called? It seemed – it was – years ago now. Sydney had changed. The fruit stall that stood in that part of King Street had long since moved off; Coles was closed and being replaced by an Eixn building; Pitt Street had been converted into a mall.

'Well, what do you say, Fran? The wife, the mistress or the man himself?' Joe's voice broke into her thoughts, bringing her back to the present. No Viet Nam now. Only the Gulf. Nicaragua. Panama. The Falklands. Lithuania. Latvia. East Timor. She sighed. 'Your guess is as good as mine, mate,' she said. 'I'd reckon it'd have to be suicide what with the way he was found up against the gymnasium door – unless we're being presented with a classic locked-door mystery. Well – I know it wasn't locked; not quite shut, indeed. But the principle's the same. If someone else did it, how'd they get in and out, leaving him in that position? Seems impossible. Yet – yet what would he do it for. Oh, I can understand some of the high flyers, in too deep, way over their heads. But there have been no rumours about the liquidity of Eixn Enterprises. No take-over bids. No paper wars. No hints of something shonky. Well, no more shonky than the usual – paying to get the ships unloaded with the least industrial disruption. Bit of creative tax accounting, no doubt. But something to die for – seems out of character for Gleixner.'

Joe Barnaby nodded his agreement. 'You're right, Fran. Could've knocked me over with a feather when I got the call. Of all that I could've expected, he'd be the last. Yet – you're right. The modus operandi is spot on for suicide. Even went to the gym to keep the mess out of the living areas. And to make it easier to clean up. Considerate bastard to the end, it seems.'

He paused, tapping his fingers on the steering wheel. The car had stopped just behind Francesca's low-slung sports model. 'Well, Fran, what do you say about coming with me tomorrow? Since we've begun by breaking all the rules, we may as well throw out the rule book altogether.'

She looked at him happily. Goddess! Just what she wanted. To be in on the ground floor of the Gleixner mystery. Who knew? She might be the one to solve it, if there was any solving to be done. 'You'd have to reckon on my answer in the affirmative,' she said, breaking into a grin. 'Is it the parents you're intending to line up?'

'Fran, Fran. You're impossible. You read me like a book. How'd you guess?' He began to open the driver's door, glancing backwards to make sure the road was clear.

'Oh – I just seem to remember some story from a while back. That her parents had more to do with his setting himself up in business than he ever wanted to acknowledge. That maybe he was "bought" in the early days. Oh, nothing sinister. Just a father wanting to make sure that his daughter got what she wanted. And twenty-five or so years of it – that's not too bad, I guess, if you go in for that sort of thing.'

Francesca Miles opened her door and leapt out on to the pavement. A wide-eyed look of innocence on his face, exaggeratedly forewarning her so that Francesca was laughing almost before he said it, Joe Barnaby called after her, 'Hey, Fran, what d'you mean? Jill and I are well on our way to ten years now. What's that? Silver – gold – copper anniversary? I can't keep up with it all. But there are some advantages in hetero-reality, you know.'

He laughed with her, and at her expression. 'Yes, I know. I know. For me. Not her. Two marriages. Mine and hers. Married men are the happiest men alive, and single women the happiest people. I've heard it before – and I believe you, I believe you.'

They stood, smiling together at their differences, one on either side of the car, leaning on the roof.

'I'll call you tomorrow, Joe,' she said. 'Just get the interview set up, and I'll come along to take notes, ask the right questions, play it straight down the line. What say we fix it tentatively for 11.30? Give you time for the press conference, me time to dig out some background for us both.'

Smiling, Barnaby watched her walk to the white car in front, open the door and charge the engine.

'We gave him everything, everything,' declared Constant Gerau as he handed Francesca Miles a cup of strong black coffee.

'He started with nothing. Nothing. And our Rosa – such a sweet girl. He swept her away, so that she could think of nothing but him. Danil this. Danil that. All the time, it was Danil. Danil. Danil. In the end – what are parents to do? We gave in, of course. Let her marry him. And gave them both a large settlement, too.'

Joe Barnaby and Francesca Miles sat in comfortable chairs overlooking the golfcourse at Bellevue Hill. Elka and Constant Gerau sat opposite, peering at them over a low coffee table that held the coffee pot from which Joe and Francesca's coffee had so recently been poured, cups (which Elka and Constant had not yet taken up, being otherwise diverted by their urgent need to convey to the visitors the justice of their position in supporting their daughter at every turn, and the injustice of Danil Gleixner in tossing her over, yet keeping everything he had built up on their early marriage gifts), and several plates piled high with sweet, luridly coloured, iced cakes. In the momentary pause of words emitting from Constant Gerau's lips, Elka Gerau added her indignation.

'Yes, we came from Central America too. Not a penny to our names. Not even ten dollars as Danil was always saying he had. We started even without that, Constant and I. With five children. Rosa the youngest. So little – only eight when we arrived. And we worked so hard. So hard. Constant selling scrap lead, tin, copper, anything he could cadge from the building sites, or the wreckers. And I – I on my hands and knees, cleaning for the rich in their houses in Point Piper. Washing, ironing, so that the rich could go to the city and get richer. Yet – eventually, we made it too.'

Constant sensed his wife had come to the end of her lung capacity for a moment, and plunged in. 'By the time she was twenty, we were comfortable. Had our own home in Edgecliffe. Oh, it was not so large. Not so large as this, but it was ours. When the time came, we paid cash. Cash. And the business had grown. I was supplying scrap throughout New South Wales. We were thinking of going interstate, maybe expanding into Wodonga. Then – this Danil came along. No money. But lots of ideas. And Rosa was mad about him. Kept sneaking out at night to see him, when we wanted her to make friends with Mr and Mrs Resnik's boy, Levin.'

'Aah, and she was sooo beautiful, my Rosa. So young and so beautiful.' Mrs Gerau leapt in, as Mr Gerau's voice halted, whilst he recalled the past.

'She could have had anyone, anyone. Any of the boys in the street. Edgecliffe Road, Watson's Bay, Double Bay, down in Point Piper, they were all mad about her. Rosa, Rosa, Rosa Gerau it was. In the houses where I had scrubbed floors and ironed shirts. In the streets where Constant collected in the early days. They were all clamouring for her. And she – my Rosa. Wasting herself on that upstart Danil.'

'Well,' said Constant Gerau as his wife took breath. 'What were we to do? Disown her? Leave her and him to make a mess of their lives? Or get behind them, build them up, so that that Danil could give her what she deserved?'

'Aah yes.' It was the second of the duo again. 'We set him up, that Danil. We did. Gave him a thousand pounds to get him started. He was employing a man and boys as apprentice mechanics, before he had even finished his own qualifications. We supported them, when he was apprenticed to his own employee, and earning nothing, nothing. We paid the rent on that first display room he talks about – that he talked about, as if it was all his own work. We paid the wages. We paid for the first car he imported. We built up that business from scratch.'

'And Rosa,' said Constant Gerau. 'It was Rosa who supported him with her love and her caring. She was so sick, so sick in that first year. Taken off to hospital two months after they were married...'

Elka Gerau rushed in, 'Yes. Working too hard. That was it. Working day and night. Taking the phone calls when they came. Tom Johnson and Millie Smith and Grace Bawden ringing, ringing, ringing all the time. "The spark-plugs won't spark" "Need a new battery." "The brake fluid's always dripping..." On and on. Emergencies night and day. Weekends. And it was Rosa who kept the business coming in, taking the calls. Answering politely when they rang in the middle of the night as if the world depended on their getting some hard-to-get gee-gaw immediately, when it could wait 'til morning.

'And she was two weeks in hospital – maybe nearly a month. Then out, and working, working, working to build up the business again.'

Inspector Barnaby took a long sip of the hot, hot coffee. He uncapped his pen. 'When did you last see him, then, Mr Gerau, Mrs Gerau. Danil Gleixner, I mean.' He looked at each, in turn, enquiringly.

They hesitated. It was almost, but not quite, imperceptible. 'Why – why – Elka, it was more than a year ago, wasn't it?' Constant Gerau sought confirmation from his wife. She was ready, now.

'Oh, yes, Inspector. He was such a wilful son – son-in-law. So uncaring, unfeeling. When he finally – finally – left Rosa, said he wasn't coming back, that the marriage – the marriage – was ended—'

There was a choking sound in her voice, as she fought to remain calm.

'Danil – he didn't visit us any more. Didn't bother to telephone or write. Cut off contact with Rosa, apart from some business matters he had to get her agreement to. He'd passed on from our circle. Didn't want to know us. Us! Us – who had given him his start in life. Why, without us, without Rosa, where would the great Danil Gleixner be? And look at him now— '

She paused, suddenly aware of where he was likely to be – the morgue, and the dissecting table.

'Well, he tried to keep it all from our Rosa. Wouldn't talk with her about leaving her with the business. Yet he wouldn't have the business without her, without us. He was a sly one in the end, that Danil. I was always suspicious of him, always. Didn't I always say to you, Constant. . .'

What Mrs Gerau had always said to Constant, Francesca Miles and Joe Barnaby were not to learn – at least not at that moment. Constant Gerau quickly interrupted her, spreading out his hands towards the other two. 'A year, maybe eighteen months ago. When he moved permanently to the Skye Apartments and that – the other one. He was probably ashamed of the way he had treated Rosa, treated us. Couldn't look us in the face. Just sneaking around the town, making sure to avoid Elka and me. Afraid of what we might say to his face, if we saw him. . .'

'And afraid of what they might do?' thought Francesca, musing as she sat back in the firm but comfortable chair, placing the cup of coffee, still full, on the side table. Was this old pair – either of them – capable of bringing to an end the life of the son-in-law they had not really wanted, had set up in business and now saw deserting their daughter and making her life miserable. Would either of them shoot – to kill?

Comparing notes afterwards, as they walked companionably up the short, though steep and winding, path from the house to Bellevue Road, they wondered aloud whether Elka Gerau and her husband might be so much on their daughter's side as to end the life of the man who had taken their money, then left her for a younger – much younger – woman.

'Alibi's not much good, if it comes to that,' said Joe Barnaby. 'Each backs up the other – but if they're in it together, or one suspects the other did it, doesn't count for anything.'

'I guess it depends on the gun, Joe. Where it came from. Whose it is. Fingerprints. Wonder if either of them had been in the penthouse before Rosa and Danil broke up? Hardly seems likely that they'd visit the pied-à-terre of their son-in-law and his mistress. Unless he owned it before he took up with Elizabeth Prince.

Anyway, if there's no excuse for their fingerprints at the apartment, then they've got to be suspect.'

She opened the car door and shouted to Joe across the roof, 'How's the lab. going with the analysis of prints and fibres from the scene? And what about the weapon?'

'I'll check up when we get back,' said Barnaby, climbing into the car. 'But who d'you say we should put next on the list, Fran, for interrogation? Friends and neighbours; the "good" daughter; the wayward son. . . ?'

Francesca heaved a private sigh of relief. It looked as if she was in for the duration.

IV

In which the Good Daughter Speaks

The man of wealth usually doles out his gifts,
so you must convince him you have no interest
in his money and at the same time get him to
give it to you.

'PARKSON VENTURA IS running at Randwick today,' said Francesca, looking at Barnaby over the yellow racing pages of the *Telegraph Mirror*. Joe Barnaby grunted and kept his head bent, typing with two fingers on the battered machine which sat squatly on a table to the left of his desk.

'Thought you might be interested.' Francesca was insistent. Joe's eyes concentrated harder on the white page in front of him, trying to make sense out of the 'facts learned so far'. He counted them off, one by one, in his head.

<u>Gun</u> – inconclusive: unlicensed; ordinary Colt 38, able to be bought from the most unsophisticated gunshop. Inspector Barnaby had several officers going around to the gunsmiths in the city, checking their records, going through their files; they had come up with nothing – yet.

<u>Fingerprints</u> – Danil Gleixner's alone found on the gun; his and what Barnaby took to be those of Elizabeth Prince (she was still under sedation and police guard at Point Piper, her fingerprints yet to be taken and tested) all over the apartment; maid's prints everywhere they should be, even on the edges of the skirting board where she had obviously bent down to dust and left

31

a thumb print or two by mistake; several sets unknown (the daughters'? the son's? a hired assassin? an unknown cat-burglar? the electrician?). But nowhere those of Rosa Gleixner or either of her parents. Yet – didn't prove anything, reasoned Joe Barnaby: gloves (cotton, wool, rubber, hastily fashioned with Gladwrap) are readily available to anyone; easily donned; capable of concealing fingerprints anywhere – doors, door knobs, light switches, smooth surfaces, rough surfaces, mirrored surfaces... guns.

Alibis – Rosa Gleixner's nothing to speak of: she cleared customs at around 10.15 a.m. and could have made it to one of the telephones in the concourse before travelling back to the city, to hoax the maid into haring off to the Royal North Shore Hospital and a sister who wasn't there, hadn't even been in an accident. Okay, she checked in at Rose Bay as she said she had, round about 11.30 a.m. But she hadn't been seen by anyone since then (at least, not as reported to the police) until she swept into the apartment at Skye, to confront Francesca Miles and Joe Barnaby. Had told her maid and butler she was going to rest. Sleep off 'jet lag'. Could easily have made an earlier trip to Skye, then returned, loudly, when the body whose demise she had brought about had long since departed.

Suzanne Williams, the Duchess Aziza and Alyssia had been helpful: answered all the questions put to them; did their best to remember times and places, departures and meetings. But to a woman they were vague about Rosa Gleixner's precise movements through customs. They had walked together toward the queues where they presented their passports, only to be divided by the officials pointing them, one to one immigration officer, the next to another. Rosa had gone through first, and met them outside the main doors, near the taxi rank. She had been waiting there patiently. And no, said the Duchess; no, said Alyssia; and no said the woman Williams (as intoned the report of the detective sent to do the interviews), Rosa Gleixner was not breathing as if she had been running – from a swift scoot to the telephone or anywhere. She was her usual self: large, brassy, bouncy, ebullient. (They didn't use quite these words; but the detective got the picture. As did Joe Barnaby.) So – could mean something. Could mean nothing.

Where was he? Ah, yes. Alibis: Elizabeth Prince – one of his officers had done a run-through of her movements, according to the version she had presented on the first day, before sedation and the private Point Piper nursing home. Mirroring her account, she left the apartment at 9.02 a.m. Drove to the city. Parked at Eixn Enterprises. Walked through Grace Brothers and Centrepoint, lingered in David Jones, on the first and second floors, took the elevator to the top floor. Yes, said Suzanne Pleasamore to the gentle questioning: we met at 10.30 a.m. at the restaurant for coffee. Well – yes, she agreed (she was polite, co-operative, helpful – like the others), could have been 10.35 a.m. Give or take a few minutes on either side of the half hour. And, said the good officer's report – it was only what Inspector Barnaby expected – yes, a telephone (indeed a row of them) stood immediately outside the elevators, along the wall, just to the side of the entrance way to the coffee shop. Simple enough for Elizabeth Prince to set herself up in the booth farthest from the eye-range of anyone alighting from escalator or elevator, or already ensconced at a table, and put through a quick telephone call, voice disguised but ordinary, to Skye Apartments to put off the maid. Why, Danil Gleixner could have been dead then, killed before she left home.

Joe Barnaby sighed. Could be even more wide open when they'd interviewed the others. And who else might there be gunning for Gleixner? Who knew what enemies he might have made (would surely have made) in the business world: the above ground world of cut and thrust on the stock exchange, the bloodless coup of the corporate raider; the underground world of evading customs or making deals, secret commissions, secretive enterprises.

And the time of death? Wouldn't you just know in a case like this one, there'd be something to interfere with the 'pat' answers he usually obtained from an autopsy. (If science and medicine could provide precise answers to anything.) Time of death difficult to determine, said Dr Trembath. 'Come, come, Joe. He left the electric heater on. Buggered us up a bit. Time of death? Could be 9.30 a.m. Could be 10.00 a.m. Could be 12.30 p.m. or so – just before he was found. Heater left on? Can't blame my technology for that.'

Someone left it on.

'Penny for them, Joe.' Francesca had been looking over his shoulder, reading his report. She took up the papers supplied by forensic, and began leafing through them.

'C'mon, Joe. I'm dying to see if it wins. Parkson Ventura. It's an Eixn Enterprises' horse – otherwise known as one from the Gleixner stable. What do you say we get out to the track and follow its chances?'

Barnaby smiled ruefully. 'Okay. You win. Better than sitting here trying to get the answer out of bits of paper. Your car or mine?'

'And it's Parkson Ventura. Parkson Ventura. Parkson Ventura leading the pack. Yes. It's Parkson Ventura all the way. Parkson Ventura. Parkson Ventura. . .' There was a sharp pause. Then: 'No. No,' sounded the voice, the words almost (but not quite) falling over one another. 'Alibi is coming up on the rails. It's Parkson Ventura and Alibi. Alibi. Alibi is coming through and it's – it's – it's— '

'PARKSON VENTURA. PARKSON VENTURA. Yes – yes. PARKSON VENTURA in the fastest race of the day. May even break the record for this event. Yes. The lights are going up. It's Parkson Ventura – 1. Alibi – 2. And Junior Antrobus – 3. . .'

'Well. . .what a race. What – a – race. History has been made here today, folks. And it's in the bag for – Gleixner. . . Gleixner? Yes, the owner, I'm checking on my race cards – it's – owned by the little lady herself, Mirna Gleixner.'

There was a pause as the loudspeaker gave a squawk. Garbled voices could be heard in the race-caller's box, way above the crowd, a small part of which was now surging toward the pay-out windows, whilst the remainder screwed up their losing tickets in disgust and sat forward to wait for the next race, the next chance to find they had backed a winner.

'Well, folks, I've just checked, and Parkson Ventura is regis-tered in the name of Mirna Gleixner, younger daughter of the late Danil Gleixner (may his soul rest in peace).' (The crowd could almost feel Tom Blamey, the race-caller, place his hand reverently over his heart, bowing his head for what passed as one minute's silence at the race track.)

'And – she's here with the man who's made an honest woman

of her, Charlie Tyson from the West. So it's Parkson Ventura, number one, owned by Mirna Tyson. And here she comes. Here she comes folks, greeting Parkson Ventura and the jockey, Smiley Smithson, in the paddock.'

The voice halted for a few moments as its owner gazed down on the scene. The sun, shining. The distinctive colours of the jockey glittering in the light. The blue sash. Roses. A kiss for the horse and a peck for the jockey. Charles Tyson there, too, basking in the memory of the roar from the crowd, soaking up the cheer that went up as weights and times were posted. Parkson Ventura had it. Looked like a sure thing for the Melbourne Cup. Charles Tyson didn't want to anticipate – but he knew, as he had recognised when he first got to know Mirna Gleixner, that his new wife had a good eye for the horses. And she had picked right when she had taken this one from her father's stables, and lodged it in her own, the first of what she (and he) intended to be a string of thoroughbreds, taking on the big stables around the country – around the world. Charles Tyson let his mind swoop into the future. A future of horses and cups and ribbons and wins. And money. And boy, did he need it...

'Arrived Monday morning, if you must know.' It was Charles Tyson who spoke. Francesca Miles and Joe Barnaby sat opposite him, across a large table in a private room, just off the private members' stand. Not wanting to pass up the chance of interviewing the honeymooning Mirna Gleixner Tyson, they had arranged, with a little difficulty, a place where notes could be taken, they could not be overheard, and another piece in the jigsaw could be filled. Charles remained belligerent at this imposition, as he saw it; never mind that there was a murder – or suicide – investigation to complete; never mind that others' time was just as important as his, or more so; just as valuable as his, or more so, thought Barnaby.

'Yes, Mr Tyson. Perhaps you would allow Ms Gleixner – pardon, Ms Tyson – to answer the questions.' Detective Barnaby spoke quietly, but firmly. Mirna Tyson did likewise.

'Yes, Charles, just let me speak for myself. I may be your wife, but you're not my keeper. I love you – but I don't love you in place of me. I'm perfectly capable of running the winner of that last race, as you could see, and I'm equally capable of answering whatever questions the sergeant and his constable here might wish to put to me.'

'Inspector. Inspector Barnaby, and my assistant,' Joe Barnaby had already introduced himself and Francesca Miles. He did it again, unruffled by the young woman's slightly imperious manner, then continued: 'And you've been staying – where?'

'Intercontinental,' said Charles Tyson, still pugnacious.

Mirna barely looked at him. 'We've been at the Intercontinental since Monday, Inspector.' (She had decided to give him his correct title, Barnaby noticed. He wondered what she would call Francesca. Or if she would direct any answers to her at all.)

'And your movements since then?' he asked, inclining his head, slightly, in enquiry.

She reeled it off, as if she had learnt it by heart. Charles Tyson sat, leaning forward, as if he was hovering over her words, willing her to get them right. ('Funny bloke altogether,' thought Francesca. 'Some odd business going on there.' Whether it had anything to do with the locked gym mystery, as she and Joe now called it, as a sort of code-word between colleagues, was another matter. 'But worth keeping an eye on,' she said later, to Joe. 'He's up to no good. Exactly what – well, you and I can sort that one out as well – or in the course of.' Barnaby again congratulated himself on bringing Francesca in on the investigation. Like to bring that Charles down to earth. Didn't want to spoil his honeymoon, but it was beginning to look as if Charles himself might have done that – or that he was afraid his wife-of-a-week had done it for him.)

'Why Inspector,' said Mirna coyly, inclining her head slightly, her cheeks growing pink, 'I think – I mean – we spent the better part of both days indoors. Our suite. Checked in about 4.30 p.m. and had dinner about 9 o'clock, alone. Then Tuesday, well, we slept in. Room service came up about 12.30 p.m. – 1.00 p.m. Just – strawberries, it was. And brie and camembert.'

It came out in a rush.

'We – came down for afternoon tea. . .And then we took a walk along the Quay. Right up to the Opera House, then along the Domain path. Walked right up to the Art Gallery from Mrs Macquarie's Chair.'

'Had dinner at one of those restaurants between William

Street and Oxford Street,' butted in Charles Tyson, determined to make his presence felt.

Francesca Miles was regarding them closely whilst maintaining a faraway look on her face. 'You didn't drop in to visit your father?' She shot the words directly at Mirna, who gazed at her with wide open eyes.

'No, no we didn't. Daddy – Daddy had just got back from Perth anyway. He came to the wedding, of course, and stayed to do some business. At least – that's what I – we – understood.'

Before she could continue, Charles Tyson forced himself into the discussion once more. 'Just what are you trying to say?' he demanded, glaring at Francesca, his face suffused, the veins on his forehead knotting slightly.

'Mirna did everything right by her father. She was good to him. Did whatever he told her to do. Well – until she decided to marry me. And that was after years of trying to please him. But it was never enough. Daniella was the one, whatever she did she was in the right. That Tomas – he never tried, and look where it got him – a drunken bum, pouring shit on his father at every opportunity. As for Mirna. Well, Mirna, my love, you tried. But nothing was good enough.'

He paused, the belligerence coming back into his voice. 'And Mirna loved him. Loved her father – even though— ' the words came out at a rush, 'he didn't deserve it. Selfish bugger.'

'Charles.' Mirna's voice sounded almost harsh in the momentary silence. 'Charles. You know he – he was a generous man. It was just – just – that he was always so busy after I was born. He didn't have any time for me, *not* because he was selfish. He had to build up the business.'

Her voice faded slightly, as if memories of the past were intruding into the present.

'Oh, come on, Mirna.' Charles Tyson appeared to have lost his earlier resolve to be discrete and controlled. His resolution to protect Mirna from an inquisitive Inspector of Police and his offsider had evaporated in the heat of what appeared to have been a difference of opinion between the honeymooning couple for some time.

'You know he was interested only in himself. And Daniella. Well – if he was interested in anyone else, it was her. You know that. Gosh, I've had to put up with hearing you whine about it often enough.'

Hardly seeming to realise how badly he had fallen out of the role of happy-young-honeymooner, doting on his young-and-beautiful (and defenceless) wife, Charles turned toward Barnaby, the words thrusting themselves from his mouth. 'You know how these Latin Americans are. Everything for the first-born. Nothing left for the rest. For Tomas it was bad enough. He was the first-born male, but missed out on all the glory that was heaped on Daniella. God! The man thought the sun shone out of that girl's rear end.'

He inclined his head towards his wife, who had gone white – whether with anxiety or self-pity, Francesca Miles was not sure.

'And you – you, my love, the last of the three. Didn't have a chance. Not a bloody chance in hell.'

'Charles.' Mirna's voice was sharp, and high pitched. 'That's – that's just not true. You know he doted on me. Gave me Parkson Ventura as a wedding present. You know it was his most prized possession. He wouldn't have given it to me – to us – if he hadn't cared.'

She turned toward Francesca Miles, as if sensing that a woman would understand, be more likely to be on her side.

'You must realise that my father – my father was so bound up in his business. Didn't have a lot of time for any of us children. He had to – he had to make a living. Keep the business going. He did it all for us – all for his family.'

Charles Tyson had begun to drink heavily. His upturned glass was emptied, righted, and filled from the champagne bottle standing next to his left hand. 'Look here, Inspector,' he butted in, reverting to his earlier role of guarding his wife from police interrogation. 'Why all these questions. We've told you all we know. And if you're wondering why we're out here, accepting the trophy so soon after his death – Mirna's father's death – well. . .it's as he would have wanted it, isn't it Mirna?'

He swept on, not expecting her to respond.

'You must know him by reputation, Inspector. Danil Gleixner lived high and fast. Nothing stopped him – well – until now. And he wouldn't have wanted his children to stand sobbing on the sidelines when he went. That'd be the last thing on his mind.'

Mirna gave a small nod, agreeing with Charles on this point at least. Charles Tyson rushed on: 'And – and Mirna'd be the last to harm him. Why, there was nothing in it for her.'

He paused. 'You must have known he thought I was after his money. Thought that was why I wanted to marry her. Everyone knew it. The gossip columnists practically screeched it from the rooftops.'

A gasp from Mirna diverted him for a moment. 'Oh, come on Mirna.' The harsh tone was back.

'He thought I was the male equivalent of a gold digger, whatever it is. Gigolo, I expect. Though god knows I don't – didn't need his money, or his time, or his backing. You must know, Inspector— '

The Tyson cheeks appeared to puff out in childish pride.

'We've got the biggest spread in the whole of Western Australia. Challenges any land holders anywhere in Australia, for that matter. The Queensland Kidsons have nothing on us. *I'm* not dependent on a Danil Gleixner for anything – anything.'

He hesitated, the redness which suffused his face spreading to his throat and seeming to interfere with his vocal cords. Barnaby and Francesca Miles sat silent, waiting for the tirade to end, sifting through the information for what it might disclose not only about Charles Tyson and Danil Gleixner, but about the suicide-murder riddle that still confronted them.

'Well, so what if he wasn't interested in sheep and wheat. It's us that've raised Australia to what it is. Not those jump-ins from Asia and Central America who think they're contributing so much to the country. I tell you Inspector, and you— '

He looked at Francesca, seeking to impress his logic upon her with equal fervour.

'It's the farmers who've made this country great. The wheat and the sheep and the cattle. That's what built Australia from the first, and it's what'll keep Australia in there, up on the world markets and strong. A world power. That's what we'll be. And it'll all be due to us. Us. The farmers. The ones who've worked day and night. No understanding from the little men of this world – the tradesmen, the mechanics, the carpenters, the little men.'

Charles Tyson had swung into a speech that he had obviously given at other times, to other audiences. Mirna had clearly heard it before. She reached out gently with one hand, laying it on his arm. With the other hand she removed the champagne bottle from his reach, over toward Francesca who sat opposite, to Charles' right. (It was an almost futile gesture, Francesca noted: the bottle was almost empty.) 'Charles— '

'Oh, all right Mirna. I know you think he's wonderful – was wonderful. But he gave you nothing, nothing. Why, when you wanted to invest in my family's company, what did he say? That Australia had to move with the times. Primary industry was on its knees. On its knees. Well, I ask you. What did he know about it? Probably never seen a sheep-dip in his life. Wouldn't know what crutching was to save his life.'

His voice halted suddenly, deflated.

'Anyway, Mirna. He's gone. And we've got Parkson Ventura.'

He looked at his wife, who had grown very still. 'And probably little else, if I know your father. Needn't even go to the reading of the will.' His words were slurring, now. His hand reached for the bottle, grasped, and found nothing but air. 'Left it all to Daniella, I'd reckon. Even if she was a bit on the outer lately.'

He nodded sagely toward Francesca Miles, including Joe Barnaby in the roll of his head.

'Yep. I'd guarantee Mirna had nothing to kill him for, if that's what you're thinking. If we're – if she's going to get anything out of all this, being Danil Gleixner's daughter for twenty-four years, then it'll be through Parkson Ventura.'

Charles Tyson put a limp arm along the shoulders of Mirna Gleixner Tyson. 'She loved him. She was good to him. And what does she get out of it? Parkson Ventura.'

He sneered, almost, into his new wife's face. 'But not a bad deal when you come to think of it.'

He turned back to the others: 'And she didn't have to kill him to get it. He'd made the horse over to her the day before the wedding. And we've got the next Melbourne Cup winner on our hands.'

V

In which Danil Gleixner's Deals are Discussed

*Man does his warring with an impudent disregard
for the written rules of civilised combat. He will take
the fortress or ravish the citadel, only to abandon it
and go on to some other mischief.*

'JOE! HERE I am, thinking I'm wise in the
ways of the world, but I sure don't know half of it, if this file
has anything to do with it.' Francesca Miles waved a bulging
manila folder in Joe Barnaby's direction.

With a friendly wave born of the comradeship between
women and a mutual recognition of workers who enjoyed their
jobs, she had walked in past Jill Maddicks, the receptionist, who
had grown accustomed to her appearances. She had spent Thursday afternoon at the Broadway offices of the *Sydney Morning
Herald*. A friendly librarian is always an asset, and she and
Madge Armytage, chief librarian at the *Herald*, had a mutual
respect for one another. Their friendship stretched back to
Francesca's schooldays, when Madge ran the school library and
frequently kept it open, providing much needed afterschool
care for Francesca and one or two others whose mothers had
jobs precluding them from 'being at home' at the close of the
school day. Francesca read voraciously, to the delight of both
her mother and Madge Armytage. And it was from Madge she
had learnt her appreciation of film.

Slapping the folder down, Francesca Miles drew up a chair to the perimeter of Joe Barnaby's desk.

'Look at this. It goes right back to those lowly beginnings we keep hearing about. The story of the ten dollars in the pocket – or, rather, ten pounds. Then there's the occasional dirt: couple of occasions of being picked up for going over the speed limit, or above .05; and trying to pay his way out of it.'

She paused.

'But that was before he became "respectable", attending government and business receptions. Having Prime Ministers and Premiers and Ministers for Trade and Business slapping him on the back and telling the world how fortunate was Australia for having him, the brave-man-of-business, leading the economic boom, then taking Australia into economic recovery.'

She had been rifling through the cuttings, and glanced up, cynically. 'Of course they omitted to acknowledge that it was Danil Gleixner and his ilk that got the country into the parlous economic situation in the first place, carrying on like corporate cowboys, borrowing overseas at no expense to themselves, adding to the foreign debt that you and I – and the woman struggling on supporting parent's pension – have to pay for. And it wasn't only the politicians who failed to see. The media's been just as bad, lauding these types as heroes.'

Joe Barnaby nodded.

'Well, Fran, at that rate we may as well close up the file, say thank you to whoever did it, whether himself or someone else, appreciate the favour and get on with chasing up the deaths that matter.'

'Joe, you're right!' she grinned. 'Seriously, though, there are deaths that matter far more, and the police should be putting resources into them – the women and children— '

He broke in, 'True. True, Fran. But we mostly know who it is in those cases: husband; father. Sometimes wife. Sometimes mother. Usually years of bashings. Rape. Sexual interference with the children, and she's just found out about it, so turns around and kills him. Not much the CIB or Homicide can do in those cases, except arrest and prosecute.'

He paused, taking a mouthful of coffee he had poured from a primitive percolator on the ledge behind him and motioning at her with questioning eyes.

At the shake of her head he went on.

'And anyway, you're just as intrigued by all this as I am. You want to know what happened, too. Suicide. Murder. Who dunnit, as they say.'

She agreed without speaking, drawing one of the sheets from the file and jabbing at it with her forefinger. 'There's lots here the man might have died for,' she said. 'Deals, reneging on deals, entering into "arrangements" with the city fathers, then having the rug pulled out from under his feet when some councillor feared for his back. Gleixner engaging in "pay backs" for deals gone sour. Gleixner using "persuasion" where previously money had changed hands for quick council approval.'

'But it was always suggestion and rumour, Fran.' Inspector Barnaby grimaced. 'There was nothing concrete. People clammed up when it came to actually talking to police – to us. They'd confirm stories with journalists. Give them the "reliable source" (or two, or three). But when it came to any possibility of standing up in court, swearing on the Bible. . .Different matter.'

'Yep,' said Francesca shortly. 'But look at this one. At least they got him to court on this one. Oh – nothing criminal, but his business practices exposed for all the world to see, anyway.'

Joe Barnaby ran his eye down the columns of newsprint. It was a report of an action taken in the New South Wales Supreme Court, by a group of lessees of Samuel D. Roast 'n Ribs. The chain had been established some ten years before the court proceedings, by an American entrepreneur who had built up the business along 'family' lines. The lessees were usually wife and husband who had recently retired and taken with them a large amount of superannuation, so were looking for some venture they could buy into, to work at for another ten years or so, until they wanted to move to the Gold Coast, or Batemans Bay, or wherever by that time it had become popular for retirees to move for golf, leisure, long (or short) walks, reading, gossip, a place to drink tea or coffee (sometimes brandy, scotch or beer) and reminisce.

Contrary to what was often seen as standard American practice, the entrepreneur, Samuel D. Straughen, had not sought to screw every dollar from the lessees, take every smart trick. Although the arrangement was that they lease the name Samuel D. Roast 'n Ribs, the shop in which each individual business was carried on, the goodwill arising out of the trade and quality of the fast food product, it was accepted by all lessees and Samuel D. Straughen that leases would automatically be renewed at the end of each term (barring outrageous conduct, or conduct detrimental to the business, which no one had ever engaged in, not at Samuel D. Roast 'n Ribs), and when husband and wife wanted to move on to total retirement, they would be able to 'sell on' the lease to an incoming couple. The latter had to be acceptable to Samuel D. But traditionally this had not been difficult: the arrangement had worked since its inception without approval being withheld. (Probably because trust had developed between the parties, pride in the product and a desire to ensure that one's shop continued in the same tradition, albeit one was no longer there, as part of the great Samuel D. Straughen team.)

Samuel D. came regularly to visit his Australian stores, attending at each and taking a personal interest in the presentation, the customers, the decor, the trade. Couples who had moved on were invited back, on a regular basis, to the yearly reunions organised by Samuel D. Straughen's Australian operations. They were all a part of one big, happy family.

Until Samuel D. died. And Samuel D.'s Roast 'n Ribs was sold. To an arm of Eixn Enterprises.

Danil Gleixner was not one for 'one big happy family', it seemed. At least, not where business was concerned. He had smartly put an end to the arrangement whereby leases were automatically renewed or 'sold on'.

Lessees had been disturbed at the news, which seeped through slowly as each lease renewal came up. Couples approached Danil Gleixner individually, seeking special consideration. Demanding that he honour the arrangement between themselves and Samuel D. Begging that he listen to the reasons why they should be allowed to continue under the rules of the old order, rather than be dictated to by the regulations of the new regime.

Seeking was to no avail. Demanding was worse: Danil Gleixner did not hear demands. Or, if he did, his anger at the temerity of those whom he considered to be minions, irrelevant in the Gleixner chain of command, wholly unnecessary to the continued building of the Gleixner fortune, of no value in expanding further the power of Eixn Enterprises (and Danil Gleixner) – was monumental. If anyone got past the series of secretaries and offsiders who protected him from contact with those with whom he wanted no contact, they received a diatribe of abuse, a barrage of profanity.

Tom Robards was one who fought his way into the presence: he waited outside his offices daily, leaving Jen Robards, his wife, in charge of the store (with the assistance of the three children as school and university lectures permitted). He was desperate. So was she. The children knew how much it meant to their parents. Every penny they had, had been sunk into their Samuel D. Roast 'n Ribs lease. If they lost it, they lost their chance of a secure retirement at Coffs Harbour, a retirement that had been planned long ago, when they had honeymooned there, lazily lounging on the beach, eating the bananas and kiwi fruit grown in plantations that ran almost down to the water's edge.

The only reward Tom Robards received for his vigilance was a shouting match with Danil Gleixner, who was quickly swept away in his large white Mercedes. And for Robards there was a heart attack, the first of two which were to severely hamper his ability to work in the shop he and Jennifer had made their life for the past eight years (and one lease renewal). Heart attacks which were to impair his health, restricting his former golfing and tennis prowess. (Oh, he had not dashed around the court like a nineteen year old. But he had kept up with friends of his own age, and ten years or so less. No more, 'after Gleixner' as the family came to call it.)

After Gleixner, Tom Robards had taken to writing begging letters. Like the seeking and demanding, the begging was met with a brick wall. Impervious to the pleas, Danil Gleixner continued as planned, to terminate the leases.

As the knowledge seeped around the state, then from state to state, the lessees took collective action. Tom Robards was to the fore, establishing a 'Fight Gleixner' group. A fighting fund had been set up. At the thought of losing everything, lessees donated whatever they could, aware that if they lost the battle a few extra dollars meant little. If what they had could be used to beat Gleixner, then it would be. If they went down, then it wouldn't be for the want of courage.

Meetings were held. Strategies discussed, discarded. They sought legal advice. And so an action was launched against Eixn

Enterprises, based on the principle of custom and business practice: Samuel D. Straughen had 'sold' leases on the understanding that they would be renewed and able to be sold on. This, the argument ran, was the basis upon which Danil Gleixner had bought the business, whatever the formal terms of each lease arrangement. The action began its long, winding path through the courts.

Meanwhile, practical action of another kind was also being taken. The chain of shops (as the name indicated) sold roast chicken, whole or pieces, and roast ribs. (Together, of course, with the ubiquitous french fries.) Along with the chain, Danil Gleixner had bought cattle stations in Queensland and Western Australia, and chicken farms around the country. Indeed, it was the cattle stations that had first appealed to Gleixner, intent on expanding his empire not only in capital but also in square miles.

The entire enterprise was highly profitable: just as Samuel D. Straughen had had a huge, permanent market for the meat grown on the stations and farms, so too did Danil Gleixner. It was the perfect arrangement: thousands of chickens grown by small-time farmers, who were dependent upon Eixn Enterprises for their livelihoods. He owned the land and equipment; they grew the chickens and sold them to his stores; cattle stations in Queensland and Western Australia, managed by men who knew to whom they had to answer, and that their production quotas had to go up each year, or Danil Gleixner would have more than something to say. There was a large export market for cattle, and Eixn Enterprises sold meat through Roast 'n Ribs stores in New Zealand, Europe and the United States, and the stores opened in China and (even more recently) Moscow. But the domestic market was a vital part of the business.

The lessees knew this. They sought alternative sources. They had no desire to harm the chicken farmers working on what were now Eixn farms. They had no personal problem with the managers of the beef runs in Western Australia and Queensland. But they had to survive and to survive they took the only steps they could see as open to them. Legal action might succeed, but one could never be sure. Anyway, it might be too late for many of them, whose leases were coming up for renewal month by month: they'd at least be thrown on to the dole or age pension, and obliged to give up their livelihoods, their satisfaction in running a business and making a profit. They set up a committee to seek out alternative sources of chicken, ribs and steak.

Gradually, the actions of the Fight Gleixner group began to have an effect on the value of Eixn Enterprises. When chicken became an everyday Australian dish rather than, as some years before, a 'treat' for Sunday lunch or dinner with roast potatoes, roast pumpkin, sweet potatoes, parsnip, swede, peas, beans, carrots, brussels sprouts. . ., hundreds – perhaps thousands – of 'ordinary Australians' went into the chicken-farming business. Not all of them were controlled by Danil Gleixner. Those who weren't, welcomed a new outlet. They were enthused by the orders coming from Samuel D. Roast 'n Ribs stores. So much so that they grew more chickens, put up more sheds, or larger sheds. And the cattle stations which had previously been out of the Samuel D. Roast 'n Ribs market welcomed the new trade. Cattle numbers on their runs shot up, just as cattle numbers on Eixn Enterprises stations declined. Danil Gleixner fumed and shouted. But there was nothing he could do whilst a lease was running. The lessees were entitled to take their meat from other sources. (That was another arrangement that Samuel D. Straughen had allowed to continue when he owned, controlled and ran the business with his 'happy family' touch. No lessee had subverted the sales arrangement between the stores, the cattle stations and the farms when Samuel D. was alive.)

As Eixn Enterprises suffered, the legal action proceeded through the system. Danil Gleixner was trapped: he wanted to launch an action against the lessees, suing them from failing to abide by the arrangement they had had with Samuel D. Straughen, to take chickens and ribs only from him. Yet in doing so, he would have to argue custom and business practice, rather than formal terms of any agreement: precisely the argument the lessees were seeking to use against him. For himself to use it would be tantamount to admitting there was good cause for accepting 'custom and business practice' as essential to the enterprise; how could he limit this to his own desired arrangement – that the lessees be bound to buy (and to sell through the stores) only from *his* chicken farms and cattle stations, whilst cutting out the arrangement the lessees sought to enforce – that the lessees be entitled to have their leases renewed, or to sell them on to approved purchases, the approval being a matter of course?

Ultimately, the Fight Gleixner group won. At first instance, Justice Quinlan had said no, the formal terms of the agreement took precedence over any presumed or alleged custom or business practice. Having begun the action, there was no point in stopping now, the lessees agreed. They appealed. A full court comprising Justices Stevens, Nimmo and Donchen was unanimous in overturning the decision of the court below.

Yet it was too late for Tom Robards. Despairing, worn out, distraught at what he saw as his business failure, distressed that (as he saw it) he had brought his family into penury, Justice Quinlan's rejection of the lessees case was the final indignity. Two days after he disappeared, days in which his family's anxiety was heightened beyond even that it had reached throughout the entire history of the matter since Samuel D. Straughen had died and the business been taken over by Eixn Enterprises, the body of Tom Robards was found in his old Holden car, parked on a deserted road leading into Kuringai Chase. A garden hose remained attached to the exhaust pipe, and led into the car at the rear window. He had strapped his body into the front seat, as a final message to himself not to change his mind. A note to Jen Robards, saying he was sorry but he could not go on, apologising for the distress and monetary loss he had caused her and the children, was by his side.

The last item in the Tom Robards section of the file was a series of notices from the Death Notices section of the *Sydney Morning Herald*. The Fight Gleixner group had a large notice, bounded by thick black lines and a two-inch deep white, blank space at top and bottom. Individual couples, other lessees, had inserted their own regrets at Tom Robards' passing. Various arms of the Robards' family had listings in one or other of the four columns devoted to him. And in addition to their personal goodbye, a formal notice of funeral arrangements was included on behalf of the immediate family: 'The Robards' family thanks all who have been so supportive on this sad occasion, and in the weeks and months before.'

(This latter was, of course, a discrete reference to 'after Gleixner', or what the family now thought of as 'the Gleixner years', the time wherein they, and Tom Robards in particular, had been obliged to take up legal cudgels against Danil Gleixner.)

The notice continued, 'The funeral will be held in private, for family members only. A memorial service will be held at St Xavier's Church in Risden Street, North Sydney, on Friday 10 March. All who cared about Tom, who loved and supported him are welcome.'

'Flowers are appreciated,' it went on, 'And those who wish to make a donation to the Fight Gleixner Fund know that Tom would appreciate that continuing support.'

The message ended: 'In memoriam. Jennifer Penelope Robards, Susanne Grace Robards, Robert Thomas Robards and Margaret Jessica Robards.'

There was more in the file, more deals, the recovery of Eixn Enterprises after the court battle was lost, expansion into other areas, property trust arrangements alongside the traditional base of Danil Gleixner's business, the import-export of luxury cars in which he had begun.

But Joe Barnaby did not read on. He looked up. His eyes met Francesca's. 'Horrible, isn't it?' she said. It wasn't really a question.

He nodded. 'And you think it might have something to do with this – with Gleixner's death?'

She nodded, 'It's eight years ago. I know that's a long time. But you wouldn't forget something like that. How could you, if it happened to your spouse, to your father?'

'So – what – you think it's the wife or the children – one of the children?' asked Inspector Barnaby, his eyes on hers.

'Could be. Could be, Joe,' she replied.

Not cocky. A bit subdued.

'I wouldn't like it to be. Seems with all this, maybe they'd be justified, depending upon your view of justice, an eye for an eye. All that. But – I guess one or other of them may have bided their time. Waited until it was possible to get away with it. Let the years pass without taking any steps – then— '

Her voice trailed off. He ran his finger down one of the stories, the last story, that told of the discovery of Tom Robards' asphyxiated body.

'Well, you could be right. It's something we'll have to check out. The older kids were at university then – eight years ago, and the youngest still at school. I'll put out a notice on it, for

Constable Crawshaw and Sergeant Deanes to check out. Once they've got the addresses, what they're doing now – well, you and I can look't what to do about them then. After all, could be dead, out of the country, moved state – eight years is a long time.'

VI

In which the Wayward Son Talks

A drunken man should be muzzled and handcuffed,
and weighted down in water with a red flag tied
around his neck.

'HE WAS A liar and a cheat. A thieving bas-
tard. And he turned me into a drunk.' Tomas Gleixner fell back
against his chair, a long lock of black hair flopping into his face,
his hand clutched firmly around the neck of a whisky bottle.
Glenfiddich, noted Francesca Miles. And not inexpensive. Tomas
Gleixner – or, as he was now known, Tom Eixn – lived well,
drunkard or not.

'And I'm not about to tell you where I was when someone
fired the fatal shot, as they say in the best murder mysteries. You
can find that out for yourselves. You don't need my help.'

He took a deep swig from the open neck of the bottle, fling-
ing his head back, his throat moving noisily.

'Okay, okay, chum. Keep your hat on,' said Inspector Barnaby
mildly. 'I can't compel you to answer. But you can't stop us from
asking questions.'

'Ask away then, ask away,' replied Tomas Gleixner, sweeping
out his hand in an expansive gesture that knocked a glass off the
table in front of him. It broke with a crack that echoed through
the almost-empty apartment as it hit the floor.

'But I can't tell you anything. Left home five years ago, and never been back since. Nothing to go back for.'

A self-pitying moan crept into his voice. 'Told me I had to get out and earn my own living, he did. Said he'd done it, and I should too. But why? Why when you're the son – the *only* son – of a bastard who's got it all – why should I go out and work? What'd he do it for, then, earning it all, cheating on everyone, skimping it here and there, putting in quotes that could be as low as they were, to undercut the others, because he cut corners, screwed the workers.'

He paused, taking another mouthful of whisky. 'Oh, yes. They thought the sun shone out of him. But he was deluding 'em, deluding 'em all. Let them believe they could be like he was, someday. They could build themselves up out of nothing, head up an empire. But they'd never be able to, never. He got in on the ground floor, right at the beginning of the boom. Made what he could out of 'em. Then he'd dump 'em, sure as hell, when the bottom fell out of the luxury cars and property business – as it would in the end. See it coming a mile off, if you had any sense. All the expansion couldn't go on forever. Forty cranes in the air, all perched on top of high-rise office blocks. Where're the workers coming from to put into 'em, I ask you? Fill 'em up with public servants. That's the usual cop. But what with Labor and Liberal going on about small government, getting rid of the minions by the dozens, paying 'em off with rerenchment packages. There's no one to sit behind a desk any more. Well, not enough to fill up every— '

He belched, loudly, and thrust the back of his free hand across his mouth. ''Scuse me, lady,' he said, glancing toward Francesca Miles. 'But I guess it's all in a day's work. Seen worse than me a thousand times on the streets, I guess. . .' His voice trailed off, his eyes glazing.

'Better make a cup of strong black coffee, Joe, if there's any in the cupboard.' Francesca looked ruefully at Inspector Barnaby as he got up from the couch opposite Tomas Gleixner, where she and he had sat throughout Tom's tirade.

Friday. Less than a week after Danil Gleixner's body had been carried away from the bloody gymnasium in Skye Apartments. Less than a week in which Francesca Miles and Joe Barnaby had talked with (or been talked to by) Rosa Sunny Gleixner, then told by Grant Webster of Coombs, Cooper, Candi-lune and Gzelka that that was, 'Enough thank you, my client is mine, her fortune is in my control if I can help it – and she's not going to put herself in, if there's anything to put herself in about, not if I've got anything to say about it.' Well, he had tried to stem the flow of words emitting from the mouth of the sunny – then snappy – Rosa. He had not been good at it, but at least he tried.

Only a day or so since Elka and Constant Gerau had told their side of the story, and Mirna Gleixner Tyson (without paying too much attention to the continuing intrusion of husband Charles) hers.

Francesca Miles counted them off, silently: Tomas Gleixner to go – and with the coffee poured into him, coffee now being produced by Joe Barnaby from the kitchen that was bare of food, in the way of the kitchens of alcoholics the world over, it may be possible to conduct a reasonable interview. Then there was Daniella Gleixner – the possible heir. Or at least others in the family seemed to think so. And Elizabeth Prince. Would it be a bedside interview, or would they see her, recovered, back at the Skye Apartments: depending upon her squeamishness at returning to the place of death, and the presence of Rosa Gleixner. Had the latter settled in – or left the former love-nest to the once-mistress? And what of the Robards? Would Inspector Crawshaw come up with anything worth following up – or was it another dead end?

'Coffee coming up.' Barnaby's voice broke in, shocking Tom Eixn into an upright position. The bottle had fallen from his hand, whisky seeping through the carpet near his feet. 'Wha – '

Joe Barnaby proffered the cup, extending his arm and pouring the coffee into Tom Eixn's weak-lipped mouth. He spluttered for a moment, then drank greedily, grabbing at Joe's wrist so that the cup tilted toward him, slurping the black coffee between his lips.

'So, he kicked me out. Told me to get a job. But I wasn't trained for anything.' Tom Eixn had recovered sufficiently to speak without slurring his words. He had apparently decided to co-operate, at least to an extent which he deemed appropriate. He waited, obedient, for the next question. Francesca asked it. Tom Eixn answered.

'Set myself up here a couple of years ago, after travelling around Europe. Racketed around through Greece and Mesopotamia, up through the Ukraine, then back down through China. Came home via Thailand, Malaysia and Singapore. With the obligatory stop-off in Bali, of course.'

'Been looking for work ever since?' Francesca's eyebrows rose in a question.

'Well – well, you could say that. Not many jobs going out there nowadays. I got back just after the '87 crash. And things have got worse, not better,' he said, tapping his cigarette on the ashtray in front of him. The smoke from its tip swirled upwards, then shot across toward Francesca. She moved back, thwacking at the grey, curling strand with one hand.

'Kept in touch with Mum, of course. Good old Mum. Always there when you need her. Well – in between flying off to Hong Kong for lunch, or to Paris for the weekend. Or Easter in London.'

He paused again. Barnaby, thinking it to be an apposite moment, shot the question. 'Your mother spent a few days in Hong Kong recently. She called you from there, I suppose?'

Tom Eixn glanced down at the cup he still held in his hand. 'Oh – probably. I mean – she's away so often, so many places. How'm I supposed to remember?'

'It was just after your sister's wedding – Mirna's wedding. In Perth,' said Francesca. 'You can't have forgotten that so quickly.'

'Well – no, you're right,' sighed Tom Eixn, passing a hand over his eyes. 'No way anyone could forget that. And I guess Mum and Mirna wanted to make sure they wouldn't.' He paused, then went on.

'Can you believe it? So much money wasted on such triviality. They actually flew Damon Rusden over from Brisbane to fix the flowers. Fix the flowers! God. There were flowers in the pews, flowers outside the church, flowers inside the church. Flowers on the altar. You'd wonder how Mirna saw her way up the aisle – she and Dad had to sense by some sort of telepathy where the floor was; couldn't see it. And how the priest got to the nave – well, he'd have to have extra-sensory perception, too. Thousands of dollars for flowers. Gee – I bet Mirna (or more likely that Charles of hers) is regretting they don't have the money now. Still, I guess it was one way of getting it out of Dad. He wasn't exactly liberal with the funds where his children were concerned – well, Mirna and me, that is. Daniella— '

Francesca Miles and Joe Barnaby waited for him to conclude his thoughts on Daniella and Danil Gleixner's money. Tomas Gleixner didn't oblige. He took another mouthful of coffee from the now almost cooled cup.

'You were telling us about your mother's trip to Hong Kong after the wedding,' prompted Francesca gently.

'Mmm. Well – yes. She phoned once or twice. Said the usual things mothers say to their sons – even their ne'er do well sons.'

He laughed.

'Guess I was just as much a disappointment to her as I was to him. Only son – and a rotten failure. Dad always thought – wished – Daniella was a boy. Then I came along. Right equipment, but wrong everything else. I was never good enough for him. He hardly saw me. I tried so hard to match up to whatever it was he wanted of me. But it was never good enough. Then when he hitched on to that Prince – Elizabeth – well, it was all over. No chance for me at all. And it was probably too late then, anyway. Daniella was the wonderboy-wonder woman. But even she – even she was probably going to be pushed aside when dear little Elizabeth began producing. I could see it in Dad's eye: a new wife, another family. And maybe she'd produce a boy first this time. Do what Mum never could do – set the family up *right* from the beginning. *He* was the eldest son in his family, and he expected the right thing should happen when he got married to Mum. She failed him by having a daughter first, just like I failed him by being born second. Just not good enough Tomas.'

In the last words, he parodied his father, shoving his cup back on to the table and pushing his hands down hard, one clutching at each thigh, just above his knees. He thrust his face forward, jaw jutting, eyes hard.

'Elizabeth pregnant, you say?' asked Francesca Miles, glancing at Joe Barnaby, thoughts of inheritance, wills and wads of dollars rushing into her brain.

'Well, I don't know for sure. But I do know that that's what he intended. At least, she'd been going on about it to him for ages. And he had visions of dynasties in his head. Like all the guys of his age, the ones who go overboard for someone half their age. And I – it was I who actually introduced them.'

He lifted his left arm, striking himself on the forehead in a theatrical gesture of despair.

'Why did I do it? How could a man be so stupid? There we are, enjoying ourselves at the races, me'n Jancey, and Elizabeth Prince. And *I* introduce her to my father. And he can't control himself. All over her. And she – she— '

Again he broke off. Again Francesca prompted him: 'It was in Sydney or Melbourne?'

'Sydney, then. It was Rosehill. His regular appearance at the Golden Slipper, before he'd worked himself up to the Melbourne Cup. He was running a few horses in the lead-up races, and the Slipper itself. Didn't have anything of Cup standard then. Of course, when he did get something that could actually win the Cup, what happens? Mirna talks him into handing Parkson Ventura over to her. Her and that waster of a husband of hers. God!'

'And Elizabeth Prince?' It was Inspector Barnaby this time, hoping to get more out of Tom Eixn than Tom had originally been prepared to give.

'Yes. Best friend of Jancey. Jancey Peters. Jancey was my girl-friend at the time. . .Wow! was she something. . .'

His voice trailed off.

'You're not together any more?' It was Francesca.

'No – no, not together now,' replied Tomas.

Suddenly he switched his attention to Inspector Barnaby, looking at him intently. 'So, you want to know what I was doing Tuesday morning and afternoon, when my father was being killed – or killing himself.'

He rushed on.

'Afraid I'm going to be no help to the lot of you. No alibi, you know. I was here. Here, blanked out after a drinking binge. I do it often, you've probably guessed. After all, what's a guy to do whose father disowns him, tells him to get a job, but gives him enough allowance so he doesn't need one. And when I've had it – a real soak, unable to work for a living, what does the man do? Kills himself, or gets himself killed. Probably lost all the money – our inheritance. What *I* deserve for putting up with him all these years, pretending he's a loving, doting father. And if he hasn't lost it, he hasn't left it to me. So the switch is turned off. No more money.'

He took them both in with his next look.

'Yes, you've got it. Danil Gleixner's no good to me dead. Left me out of his will. So long as he was alive, I had a chance to live on whatever allowance he gave me, at least until some new kid came along. First-born son he'd always wanted. But – dead – it's all going to Daniella.'

He scrabbled down beside the chair, hand fumbling for the Glenfiddich bottle. Finding it, he righted it and raised it to his mouth. Gurgling in his throat, the remains of the scotch disappeared. He threw the bottle to the right, where it crashed in the empty fireplace. 'Okay, that's it,' he screamed. 'I've had it. You've got enough. And you can get out. Now.'

'Happy little family, wasn't it?' Joe Barnaby was at the wheel, driving towards the Sydney Harbour Bridge from Neutral Bay. Francesca grimaced her agreement.

'Didn't like one another much at all, did they. And Danil Gleixner's death doesn't seem to have improved their liking for each other.'

'And it wasn't helpful to learn that Tomas Gleixner was free to get to and from Skye Apartments without anyone knowing where he was,' said Barnaby, stepping down on the accelerator.

'Could have been too drunk to drive,' replied Francesca slowly. 'Doesn't seem to carry his liquor well.'

'But he recovered quickly with the coffee,' said Joe. 'Seems to be one of those drunks who knows how to pace himself. I guess it's possible that he took the ferry across the harbour. Then it'd be a quick bus or train ride out to Double Bay or Edgecliffe. No need for anyone much to see him at that time. Most people at work. Skye Apartments deserted...'

'Yes, especially with the maid spirited away,' Francesca responded. 'By the way, what about checking out the maid? Is she still around?'

'I've got one of the guys – When I read that story about Tom Robards, I wondered...' He turned left, over the bridge, fumbling in the glovebox for coins. Nodding at the tollkeeper, he tossed the money into the chute and drove through.

The town hall clock showed 6.15 p.m. as they drove toward College Street and police headquarters. They heard the police siren start up as they turned into Oxford Street.

'Something urgent's come up,' said Inspector Barnaby, glancing at Francesca Miles. 'Could be something to take my mind of this indecipherable mess.'

He drew the car into the kerb, parking directly opposite the main entrance, and switched off the engine. A police officer who had clearly been looking out for him came rushing across the road.

'Inspector, Inspector.' The voice was urgent.

'Okay, Burns, what is it? No need for panic,' said Barnaby, sighing at the thought of some new matter, when he wanted to get home. Home to a hot meal and a cool hand on the brow, he thought, knowing he was sinking into cliché and unruffled by it.

'Sir. It's the Gleixner case again. Looks as if – looks as if it may have been murder. Or there's a terrific coincidence just occurred.'

'Okay, man, out with it,' Inspector Barnaby's voice was firm. 'What's happened now?'

'It's – it's Tomas Gleixner. They've just found his body. Dead. Drowned in the bath. Could be – could be an accident. The caller said there's an empty bottle of whisky next to him. But— '

'Quite see your point, Burns. But don't let's leap to conclusions.' Turning to Francesca, Joe Barnaby slapped the wheel and said: 'At least if this is murder, there's one of them ruled out this time. Without question. Cast-iron alibi.'

Francesca looked at him, mouthing the name: 'Elizabeth Prince.'

Barnaby nodded. 'Yep. She's still in hospital. No way could she be at Tomas Gleixner's Neutral Bay apartment shoving his head under water.' Suddenly, the street lights came on. Barnaby sensed the police officer who had delivered the news was lingering.

'Well, Burns, what is it? You've passed on the message. Get back on duty.' Burns looked sheepishly down at the shining caps of his regulation shoes.

'Uh, Inspector. Just one thing. I'm afraid Ms Prince isn't out of the running. She checked herself out of hospital at 4.00 p.m. this afternoon. No one knows where she's gone. Vanished into thin air.'

VII

In which Elizabeth Prince Declares Her Permanency

*A man needs the comfort and convenience
of a possession. In this respect, there is
a cosy feeling of luxury in having two.*

'THINGS ARE CERTAINLY hotting up.' Joe Barnaby spoke. He held a copy of the *Telegraph Mirror* up against his chest, front page facing Francesca Miles, so that she could read, without difficulty, the screaming headlines: 'WIFE VERSUS MISTRESS'.

Below appeared a photograph of Rosa Sunny Gleixner, hair billowing, arms akimbo, in front of the entrance to the Skye Apartments. Beside her stood Grant Webster, incongruous in his smart lawyer's suit, holding a piece of paper which, on closer inspection, appeared to be a court order.

To the left of the picture of Rosa and her solicitor a shot of Elizabeth Prince, in delicate profile, held half the page. The captions read, respectively: 'ROSA DEFENDS THE SECOND FAMILY HOME. COURT INJUNCTION KEEPING ELIZABETH OUT.' and: 'MISTRESS ELUSIVE. NOT EVEN A "NO COMMENT".'

'She's taken action to prevent Elizabeth Prince from returning to the penthouse,' said Joe Barnaby. 'And Rosa's seeking to recover the Monets and Manets, and the yacht as well.'

59

'Mmm. I see there's also a threat of action to claw back a couple of horses Gleixner put into a partnership he set up in his name and hers – Prince's, that is.' Francesca glanced over the paragraphs which sought to convey the message that this was a sordid tale of woman-against-woman, fighting over some man's property. There was not even an allusion to Rosa Gleixner and Elizabeth Prince's respective contributions to the accumulation of assets, whether they be house, penthouse, car or cars. The yacht. The business. And everything else usually built up during a marriage or de facto relationship, and in this case more, much more.

'So who's getting the books and the videos, that's what I want to know,' said Francesca, a slight frown passing across her face. (When her divorce had gone through, she had counted herself lucky in making off with the substantial library she had accumulated over her four years of marriage to Tony Sanford. A mistake she no longer spent time worrying about. Though she had had to trade the videos for the books. Not a bad negotiation, she thought, now – although she had regretted losing all the films, many of which she had critiqued for her regular column in *Filmscope*.)

'But seriously, Joe, why does this have to hit the headlines when the real world's in crisis – economy kaput (or that's what the economists and the statistics say – as well as the women who shop in the supermarkets with the rising prices), war in the Gulf, so-called peace in the Gulf, Cambodian refugees, Chinese students being ripped off—'

'Hate to use a cliché, Fran, but it sure sells papers,' Joe replied, folding the *Telegraph Mirror* and dropping it on to his desk as he spoke.

Weekend enquiries had not unearthed Elizabeth Prince's whereabouts. But, working on a hunch, Joe Barnaby had decided to sit tight. She'd turn up, ready for questioning, sooner or later. And it was likely to be sooner. If she had fallen victim to the murder-suicide-accident syndrome that appeared to be plaguing the Gleixner family, they'd have found out by now. She must be alive, and no doubt ready to talk. If only to defend herself against the notion that she was a gold-digger and homicidal maniac to boot.

Police work was often like that, Francesca knew. The public had visions of cop cars rushing thither and yon, hordes of police with guns at the ready, nightsticks poised on high. It was far tamer in reality. Oh, sure, there was detection. But often, in the case of serious crimes (or possible serious crimes) witnesses came forward with little prompting. Whether it was ghoulish curiosity or civic responsibility was never quite clear: probably a bit of both. But come forward they did, with information of varying degrees of usefulness and triviality. Often it was the trivial that was the more significant. Francesca Miles frequently thought that this was understandable: after all, the original meaning of trivia was 'three ways' or 'a place where three roads meet'. The word itself had been trivialised over the years, so it now was mostly understood as being the opposite of its origins. Significant events happened, of old, at junctions between highways just as they did at the 'ordinary' paths through a village. The place where women gathered to 'gossip' – to pass on the news, the events of the day, medical knowledge (now known as 'old wives' tales'). Just as 'mistress' had degenerated from 'woman of the house', 'controller of the domestic market', 'private sphere economist' to 'property of man' or, more accurately in these days of serial monogamy, 'leasehold'.

The phone rang. Inspector Barnaby picked it up, stated his name, and listened. 'Fine, send them up,' he said, after a long silence from his end.

Looking at Francesca, he said, 'She's here. Together with an entourage. Solicitor, barrister and some male friend. Yep. Elizabeth Prince is on her way up.'

He hitched up his trousers, felt around the back of the waist band to ensure his shirt was firmly tucked into his belt, and moved toward the door.

'Hey, Barnaby, what is this?' asked Francesca Miles, laughing. 'Don't tell me coppers – and particularly those who've been promoted to Inspector level, in charge of Homicide, are susceptible to the thought of an attractive woman? You're surely not preening because a couple of lawyers are about to step over the threshold.'

Inspector Barnaby blushed. 'Aw, shucks Fran,' he said in mock southern American accent. 'Can't blame a boy for trying.'

A knock sounded on the door. 'There, Inspector?' It was Constable Crawshaw, four figures in his wake.

'Okay, Constable. And what about some tea or coffee – tea? coffee anyone?' Orders taken, Constable Crawshaw departed to the cramped kitchen at the end of the hall. Inspector Barnaby took over the introductions.

'So, you went straight from the hospital to your mother's home in Hunters Hill,' said Barnaby. 'Do you remember which taxi company?' Elizabeth Prince shook her head. (Shouldn't be hard to find out, he thought: she sure was a knock-out, this one. Any cab driver – woman or man – 'd have to remember her.)

'I – I just had to get out of there. Couldn't bear to be cooped up any longer. Oh – they were nice – very nice to me. But it was the long days, with nothing to think about except— '

Her voice faltered. Noticeably, she squared her shoulders and went on.

'I could hardly think when I came to. They'd put me on valium or mogadon or something. Maybe something stronger, even. I didn't know where I was at first. Didn't remember what had happened, why I was there. Then it all started coming back to me. The apartment. The sun shining in. The silence. And the closed door – with the red seeping under it.'

She shuddered. Maurice Burton, who had introduced himself as her solicitor, put an arm protectively across her shoulders. She seemed to draw into herself, then looked up again. 'I can't remember much after that. There was a police officer – I don't even know how he got there – I— '

'Look, Inspector, it's still very raw for Ms Prince. Perhaps you could jot down a list of questions and we can go away and write down the answers, then get it delivered back to you.'

Francis Morrish, friend-to-Ms-Prince, spoke. Clearly, the three companions had not determined together on any plan of action, much less taken Ms Prince into their confidence. Abruptly, Simon Rees, barrister, intervened: 'Take it slowly, take it slowly, Elizabeth. Just think calmly and you'll manage.' He turned to Barnaby.

'You've got the initial statement from her, the one taken from her on the day, when she found him. You'd have checked that out by now, I'd guess. So it's only what she did after leaving the hospital – between then and now, basically.'

'Well, there is more than that,' said Francesca Miles slowly. 'We do need to check out details like – well, the will. And any arrangements made between Mr Gleixner and Ms Prince in terms of the future. The partnership, for example. The ownership of horses, a yacht and other assets.'

'Well, hang on,' butted in Francis Morrish. 'What's that got to do with you? Private matter between herself and her family – and friends. Doesn't do to take much notice of the daily rag,' he said, glancing down at the newspaper which still lay in front of Joe Barnaby, to the right of his cooling coffee mug.

'Hey, wait a moment,' said Maurice Burton, pushing himself forward on his hard-backed chair. 'I'm Elizabeth's solicitor, and I'd say it's for me to advise on what's relevant and what's not. You keep out of this, Morrish.'

'Well, wait on, you.'

Simon Rees intervened, attempting to glare down both Maurice Burton and Francis Morrish, whilst at the same time looking comforting, business-like and in control as he saw Elizabeth Prince's eyes turning toward him. 'It's for me to determine what Elizabeth's got to answer, and what she doesn't. It's not an open free-for-all here.'

'Look, Simon, we don't need to have a box-up here,' said Francis Morrish, almost visibly flexing his muscles as he spoke. 'Why don't— '

'Hey, hey, hey. Let's have a bit of calm. It's up to Ms Prince to speak up – or not. Maybe she'd be better off without you lot.'

It was Joe Barnaby who spoke, irritated at the lack of progress and the way in which his office was being taken over by a squabbling bunch of private schoolboys. At least, that was how it seemed to him. 'Perhaps we should move out to one of the rooms downstairs. More room and less heat,' he said, slapping the open palm of his hand on the desk.

'Look.' It was Elizabeth Prince, her voice sounding firmer than it had. 'I want to help. And I will. Don't worry about me, Maurice – Francis – Simon. They're not giving me the third degree. There's nothing to give me the third degree about.'

She turned back to Joe Barnaby, then glanced at Francesca Miles. 'What were you asking me again? It's difficult to keep my mind on things. I'm sorry...'

'We understand you were in partnership with Mr Gleixner,' responded Francesca, getting in quickly before Joe started on another tack. (It wasn't only 'the boys' who hadn't got themselves together before beginning this interview, she thought ruefully. Usually she and Joe were better at playing Gog and Magog, Bib and Bub, or Tweedledum and Tweedledee, or whatever duo it was that they seemed to emulate, at times.)

'Well, yes. I've got a good eye for horses. He recognised that. Gave me credit for some— ' She stopped suddenly. Almost as swiftly, she looked at Francis Morrish, who was sitting to one side, near the door. 'You always knew I was pretty good at knowing if a horse is a possible winner, didn't you?'

Almost as if surprised, Morrish looked up. 'Oh – oh yes, true, true. I remember you always were able to pick the Cup winner. Well – at least, *I* thought so.'

'There you are.' Elizabeth Prince rushed on, words tumbling out in a heap. 'Danil was going into diamonds in a big way. It was his new venture – adventure, possibly. We were looking at a stud out near Windsor. The horses were agisted there, and it was coming on to the market. We thought – we thought we'd start with Magruder and Bonne Tyndere. Parkson Ventura was going to be the big name. But – well, after Parkson Ventura went – went, well, he – we began looking into diamonds. Danil was convinced the boycott on trade with South Africa would end soon. And he had links with the South American diamond traders. We were going to Johannesburg next week— '

Her voice broke again. Simon Rees stretched out an arm, this time, to comfort her.

Absent-mindedly she brushed him away. 'The horses were in our joint names. We intended to put the stud in our joint names, too. Ours was – was a partnership. So Danil always said...'

She looked at Francesca. 'And now – now there's all this.' Her arm swept in an arc towards the *Telegraph Mirror* and its columns of reportage and speculation.

'Well, Elizabeth. We just won't let her get away with it,' said Maurice Burton, his lips firm. 'It's a valid partnership, fair and square. You've put everything into it. Given up more than five years of your life for him. Why, you could have— '

Francis Morrish jabbed him in the ribs. He stopped abruptly.

Simon Rees leapt in. 'The partnership is sound. I mean, it's legal, above board, unchallengeable. Elizabeth was no silent partner. She was a full participant in the horse-game. And the yacht's an asset of the partnership. Not a private item at all. Not the property of Danil Gleixner as such. Rosa's claim won't work. Nor for the penthouse, the paintings, the precious stones— '

'Look here, Simon. The police are not interested in hot gossip,' said Maurice Burton, his face flushing with anger. 'Just leave it – leave it. I think we've all said enough.' He made as if to rise from his chair, willing the others to rise with him.

'It's okay, Maurice. I'm happy to answer the Inspector's questions. I just want it all – all to be over. I want to go and lie down somewhere and have some peace for a while. Oh – not the hospital again, thank you. I want my own bed, my own pillow. I want to go home— '

It came out almost in a wail. But she sat straight again in her chair. 'I know quite a lot about his – our – financial affairs. That's why – that's why this is all so unbelievable. I can't believe Danil would do it – do it to himself. He's a winner, a man who'd never give up, whatever the world was saying about him, whatever hard knocks he had to contend with. Why, his big story was one of success and more success. Rising from nothing. Why would he think the stockmarket crash would touch him – why would it touch him? I just can't – can't believe he'd do such a thing. Kill himself, I mean.'

The last words came out as if she did not want to say them, as if she dreaded that in using the word 'kill' she would have to admit to herself he was dead. Danil Gleixner, who had taken her from a relatively moneyed, but oh-so-ordinary life, to the penthouse of the Skye Apartments, to joint ownership of a Windsor stud (well, almost), and a partnership arrangement involving the high-priced, magnificent sparkle of diamonds.

'Tomas Gleixner – Tom Eixn – you knew him?' Joe Barnaby was back in the picture, taking the interview in the direction he wanted. Was there anything between Elizabeth Prince and Tomas Gleixner? Anything that might give an indication of a link, a possible reason why she might want him off the scene? A reason for thinking it was not an innocent, alcoholic drowning – all in the day of Tom Eixn as it were. Rather, a planned, desired death. A need to end his life because he knew – what?

She paused, gazing toward the small, grubby window over Inspector Barnaby's shoulder. 'He – I guess we did meet once or twice. Or more. But it was a long time ago.'

'He introduced you to his father, didn't he?' said Francesca Miles, impatient to prod Elizabeth into disclosing whatever it was she knew.

'Yes.' Elizabeth Prince seemed reluctant to answer. Then it came out in a rush. 'We – we were at the races. At Rosehill. Golden Slipper. I was there with Jancey— ' Her voice almost broke.

She hurried on. 'Jancey Peters. My – my best friend. She was going with Tom at the time, Tom Eixn. We – we were together, down near the paddock. Danil – Danil had a horse running in one of the earlier races. One of the first times he had a horse at the track. We – we were walking toward the barrier. He was coming back. Tom was reluctant to speak to him, but he made him. Danil always – always got what he wanted. He made Tom speak to him, and he made him introduce us. Danil – Danil was overpowering, you know. It was hard to say "no" to him about anything. He – he got my name, got the introduction – then, he left. Just passed a few words, then left.'

She moved in her chair, the seat hard against her.

'Then – it must have been a day or so later. Maybe even the next day. I had a phone call from mother. There were bunches of roses turning up on the doorstep. I was – I had gone back to live with my mother then, because Tom had moved in with – with Jancey. And somehow Danil had found out my address, and was flooding the place with flowers. Somehow he knew I liked yellow roses. Can't stand red ones. They'd turn me off anyone. But he knew – knew I'd be smitten with them, yellow roses.'

She bent toward the desk, picking up her cup and sipping slowly.

'They arrived every half hour, the whole day. From 9.00 a.m. to 5.30 p.m. that evening. We didn't – didn't have enough vases for them. Mother sent Dad out to collect some from the neighbours. Then, when it seemed they'd stopped at 5.30 and there were no more to come, she rushed out to the Mosman shopping centre and bought cut glass to hold them. Said that if this was going to happen often, we'd not be able to keep the next doors' vases, and may as well have a stock, permanently, of our own.'

Simon Rees cleared his throat, making as if to interrupt. Before he could, Elizabeth Prince swept over him at a rush. 'She was right. They kept coming the next day. This time they started at 8.30 a.m., went through to 6 o'clock. Dad was going mad. Mum was loving it. She made excuses to invite the neighbours in for coffee or tea. So they could see. Well, in the end there was little they could see apart from the roses. It went on all week. Then finally, on Monday he telegrammed. Said he'd send around his chauffeur at 12.00 noon to collect me for lunch. I – I went. What else could I do?'

Her eyes wide, she looked first at Francesca, then at Inspector Barnaby. The other three men looked at their shoes.

'Travis took me to Pegrum's, in Woollahra. And Danil was already there. He – we lunched all afternoon, then he took me to a private showing at the Gallery. Knew, somehow, I cared about Monet. And it was that special tour of Russian Monets, that went from state to state. I – well, what could I do? He knew everything about me, what I like to eat, my favourite colours, art, flowers, films, music. Opera. He took me to *Salomé*. Then *Otello*. *Lucia di Lammermoor*. *La Bohème*. He was – he was – I thought he seemed so civil— civilised.'

Again, her voice almost broke. She bowed her head. A hand came up, brushing at her left cheek.

'Well, that's it. Some weeks later, I moved into Skye Apartments He – he visited me there regularly, all through those five years he lived still with – with Rosa, Rosa Gleixner. Then – finally I said to him it was her or me. He had to make up his mind. He made it up. He chose me.'

She could hardly keep the triumph from her voice. But – there was another emotion mixed with it, sensed Francesca. She couldn't determine what, precisely it was. But there was something . . .

'Jancey Peters. What happened to her?' asked Joe Barnaby, pursuing his own line of enquiry. 'She still with Tomas Gleixner?'

There had been no evidence of any female presence at the Tom Eixn dwelling. Still – even in his alcoholic state, Tom Eixn might have been attractive to a woman, thought Joe, glancing down at his stomach and visibly pulling in his muscles. Should get down to the gym more regularly—

'She's dead.' The voice cut harshly across his thoughts. 'But I don't want to talk about it. Danil's dead too, and I don't know what to do.'

The voice threatened to collapse into a wail again. As one, Francis Morrish, Maurice Burton and Simon Rees rose, assisting (almost pulling) Elizabeth Prince from her chair.

'That's enough for one day, Inspector, M'am,' said Francis Morrish, motioning toward the door. 'We're leaving now. If you want to speak with Elizabeth further, do so through me. Here's my card.' Before he could place it in Francesca Miles' outstretched hand, Simon Rees thrust his into it. Maurice Burton, not far behind, slapped his on the desk. The door closed.

'Want a lawyer, Fran?' said Barnaby. 'Pick a card, any card.'

VIII

In which Daniella Ruby Raises Consciousness

Men are so generous! heaps of women
can point to diamond, pearl and sapphire
rings – presents from some kind man.
And heaps of women have black rings round
their eyes. Presents from some kind man.

IT WAS A tiny terrace in Waterloo, opposite a thin grassy patch where straggling trees hid a high factory wall. Daniella Gleixner answered their ring. In jeans and flat shoes, with a large white shirt falling to mid-thigh, she seemed the antithesis of both Elizabeth Prince and her sister, Mirna Gleixner Tyson.

'Daniella Ruby,' she said, putting out her hand, first to Francesca Miles, then to Joe Barnaby, before she stepped back, guiding them into a large, airy lounge-cum-diningroom which opened out from the narrow passageway. Indicating chairs and a sofa, did they want coffee – decaffeinated or tea – herbal she asked. Doubtfully, but longing for something hot and comforting (and knowing it made questioning possible suspects so much easier), Inspector Barnaby chose the coffee. Acclimatised to rose hip, Francesca Miles asked for tea. In a short time, following a brief bout of clattering and banging in the kitchen which was off to one side, Daniella Ruby Gleixner was back with a full tray.

Readying himself for business, Joe Barnaby took a mouthful of coffee (which was not, on reflection, so bad: not so different from the real thing, he thought; and, anyway, it was hot) and crunched at a biscuit which appeared to be homemade. As he opened his mouth for his first question, Daniella Ruby was in before him.

'What do you want to know, Inspector, Ms Miles?' she asked, her hands resting gently in her lap.

'Well,' said Joe Barnaby, briefly disconcerted at her cool approach – nothing here of the voluble tirade he had become accustomed to with some of the family Gleixner; nowhere here lawyers, spouses or other hangers-on attempting to determine on the line of questioning, and what questions should be answered – or even asked; not for Daniella Gleixner initial questioning about his qualifications or capacities for undertaking this enquiry. Did this mean she *was* the one – if there was a 'one' to be, wondered Joe, looking at her even more keenly.

'Just a few standard questions, questions that have to be asked in circumstances such as this, where a death occurs unexpectedly, you understand.'

'I understand perfectly, Inspector, Ms Miles,' she responded. 'Please, go ahead.'

Forthright? practical? or calm, calculated, unfeeling and – guilty? wondered Joe Barnaby, his face remaining neutral as he had learned through his long years in the force, his time in Homicide. Never – but never – give anything away. Never let any of the suspects know you suspect them. Keep them guessing until the end. And, with family-situations such as this one (although they were not too frequent; more often there was no locked-door mystery – indeed, no mystery at all: if it was family, it was either a woman who had had one beating too many, or a man who had given one beating too many), there usually was an end, usually a time when someone confessed, or was caught out. When a crime in a family occurred, particularly where there was any money involved, property to be divvied up, shares to be determined upon, wills to be read, sons and daughters to be included in, or left out, wives and de facto wives to sort out – or over – the mess left behind, typically the crime was solved. Often by flight of the guilty one. Sometimes, though only occasionally, by his (or less often her) suicide. Generally, they felt no remorse, those who killed for greed. But hardly ever did they get away with it: well, not if the fact of the killing came to the attention of the police. Who knew how many deaths in the family were due to pushing and shoving, a pillow over a sleeping face, a carefully manipulated accident?

Francesca got in before he did. 'The Tuesday it happened. Your father's death, I mean. You were— '

'The refuge. Louisa Lawson, inner city refuge we set up last year at Glebe,' she responded. 'I do five shifts there a week, and I'm sure I was rostered on that day. I could get you the book to double check – though— ' She hesitated.

'Well, any of the women there could tell you my hours, and the days. I was on for the day, 8.30 a.m. to 5.00 p.m. We usually have collective meetings on Tuesday evenings, too. 5.00 p.m. to 6 o'clock. But – yes, we missed that day, because a woman came in who was badly beaten, and her husband had taken the children with him. She didn't know where he was; thought it'd be a murder-suicide. We were afraid it might be, too.'

'And?' Francesca wanted to be told it had worked out okay, this time. Well, as okay as it could be, in the circumstances. She got an answering nod.

'Mmm. A bully that one, but totally incompetent. The kids started to scream and cry, and he dumped 'em at Coles in the city. A customer found them sitting on the floor near the confectionery racks, with empty packets of Smarties and jellybabies around them. Having a grand old time they were, completely oblivious to the disappearance of their father.'

She smiled, tossing her head back. 'Grace – their mother – was so relieved. But she thought she'd trained them really well to eat healthy food – like dried apricots, and raisins and sultanas. Proved wrong!

Then they were sick for a week after that, and we cared for them here, until we could get an order removing the husband from the family home. Peg and Megan went back with her, as "trouble shooters", to make sure he didn't come back, crashing and bashing and carrying on. Well, when he did they stood up to him and he crawled off, tail between his legs. You can never count on it, but some of those bullies just collapse like burst balloons when you tell 'em where to get off. Pity the police don't stand up to 'em more often. . .'

Her voice trailed off as she regarded her interrogators. 'Well, yes, I guess that means you.' She found her voice again. 'Can't excuse any of you. Just as I can't – we can't – excuse any man who stands by when he knows (and they know, they all know) the guy next door's lamming into his wife, or the children. And we can't excuse any man who sits on a barstool listening to so-called sexist jokes, "the one about the woman who. . .", the one about the wife "who just needs a box around the ears". Deadly.'

'I guess I take your point, but I'm – we're Homicide,' said Joe weakly.

'Hey, I don't believe this. Joe, what're you saying,' exclaimed Francesca. 'You know most of your work involves the end result of the bar-room "joke".' He flushed, shamefacedly in agreement.

'Well, that's my work, and I guess I think it should be everybody's work – until the world's different,' said Daniella Ruby. 'I guess I learned a lot from – from experience, you could say. Homegrown experience.' They waited for her to continue.

'Yep. I guess you could say I didn't have a lot of time for my father. Oh, knew everything about the business. The tricks he got up to. The scams. The genuine work. The good deals and the shifty ones. He didn't keep anything from me. Thought I'd take it over, eventually. Couldn't believe it when I told him I didn't want it, that I didn't want anything to do with his business – well, his and Mum's business.'

She intercepted the look that passed from Joe Barnaby to Francesca Miles.

'Oh, no, nothing like that. Mum wasn't in on the wheeling and dealing, not to my knowledge, anyway. And I *know* that business. But she built it up with him. If she hadn't been there at the beginning, answering the phones, taking down the jobs, passing them on to him, keeping the books – well, there'd have been no business. And no Gleixner dynasty, either, as he wanted to call it. No one to pass the lot on to, eventually. Who'd have cared for his kids, except Mum? Who'd have made sure we got to school on time, had help with our homework, someone to do roster duty at the tuckshop and attend the Parent's and Citizen's meetings? Who'd have come to "open day" every year? Who got the stern "talking to" from the principal when Tomas got into a scrap? Who got the blame when he turned into an alcoholic? Mum. Yes, that's who. He built the business on the work she did. Without her, he'd have been nothing.'

She gulped tea from her mug, then looked steadily at both of them. 'He bashed her for it. Couldn't accept that she was central to his success. There were regular beatings. I can remember the bangs as she "fell" against the bedroom wall. Once, he shoved her downstairs, and she broke her hip – well, he broke it, I guess. She lay in bed for three days, refusing to go to hospital. I ended up ringing for the ambulance when Dad was away. He was furious when he got back, and found us being looked after by neighbours, Mum – Rosa – in hospital, in traction.'

Francesca Miles and Joe Barnaby sipped silently at their tea and coffee. Joe crunched, as unobtrusively as he could, on a biscuit.

'She left him a few times. I can remember, once, going off down to some hotel or a rooming house at Batemans Bay. She had friends down that way. But she kept coming back. He had a hold on her, as it is for most women. The pain of being apart, the feeling you're no one when you're alone – without a husband, that is. The belief that you can survive only with a male bread-winner, even if you're really resourceful, even earning most of the money yourself. She was no different, and you can't blame her for it. There were no real refuges then, not feminist run. Only the churches, and they sent you back every time. They sent her back. Priest told her her place was with him. She believed it.'

'Like another cup of tea?' Francesca rose, collecting the mugs and tray.

'What – oh, yes. Thanks.' Daniella looked up at her grate-fully. 'But – but – I've really got to get this all out, you under-stand. Oh, I'm not into the "drag down Gleixner and kick 'im out" syndrome. Not like the ones who were all over him, prais-ing him to the skies, so long as he was alive and making money. That type don't care how the money's made, as long as it keeps coming. Then, as soon as you're down, that's it. Desert. And when a man seems to have killed himself – well, what can be worse? What can seem worse to the hangers-on left behind? *They* don't want to be tainted by the thought of failure. No way. Move on to the next "successful" bastard, and keep your nose clean.

'But – I guess it may help, if you know the sort of man he

was. And why my mother – why my mother is the way she is. And Tomas. And Mirna.'

She hesitated. 'I've – we've got a new project. Advertising it around the North Shore. We've put up posters in the local shopping centres. Even got some into the local copshops.'

Daniella smiled, recalling both askance looks and fervent appreciation from the various shopowners and desk sergeants when she had approached them with the flyers and other advertising material for a women's refuge.

'We're planning on a refuge in Roseville, right in the centre of the middle-class mansions. It's going to serve the region from Turramurra down to Chatswood, and probably across to Mosman, Hunters Hill and McMahons Point. There's a real call for one, at least as a resting station until we can get the women back into their own homes, and turf the violent husband out, even if he is a lawyer or dentist or doctor, or top executive material in some high falutin' corporation.'

She stopped for a moment, her mind on the red tape the local council was subjecting the collective to, fearing a decline in the value of property in Roseville and surrounds if it became public knowledge that a lot of hairy-legged feminists had set themselves up as avengers in the community, rescuing women from their husbands. The collective was prepared for a long drawn-out battle.

The kettle was turned on in the kitchen. Francesca Miles leaned against the refrigerator, listening and waiting for the water to boil. Casually she glanced at the roster stuck to the fridge door with a magnet in the woman-symbol. Dishes. Bathroom. Lavatory. Vacuuming. Shopping. The sort of programme that appeared in kitchens around the country, particularly in group houses where friends, often related only by political persuasion or work, or sometimes coming together by advertisement or chance, lived hectic lives. Without 'the roster', dishes lay unwashed in the sink. Dust accumulated on skirting boards and table tops. Grimy marks appeared around baths and washbasins. Toilets – Francesca's eyes slid down the names allotted to the various tasks: Daniella Ruby. Suzanna Merrit. Peg Jess. Daryl Corbett. Jan Erika. That five fitted in to this small ter-

race house was a tribute to the designers and builders who filled
the early streets of Sydney with these many-roomed accommo-
dations, built to house families of six, seven and eight. Tightly
cramped, yes. But livable. Probably there were as many as four
bedrooms upstairs, and one at the front, off the hallway. A new
breed of builders had found room to put in bathrooms and lav-
atories all over the city and suburbs: often minute, certainly;
but always functional. So this was where she lived, Daniella
Ruby Gleixner, daughter – and, so far, apparently heir of the
magnate, or was it failed magnate – the books of Eixn Enterprises were yet to be sorted out.

The daughter and heir was speaking again. She had returned
to contemplating her family directly. Picking up the tray, Francesca returned with more tea and coffee, and a replenished
plate of biscuits. She had found a bit of cheese in the fridge, and
a few crackers. Daniella Ruby absently cut off a chunk, nipping
at the edges and breaking a waterbiscuit in one hand.

'I guess – I guess I'm determined to succeed on the North
Shore. Determined the collective'll get the refuge up and running.
I know how hard it was for Mum. And it seemed to get more
difficult, the richer Dad – we – got. There was so much to lose,
nowhere, really, to go. No one understood. Mum was locked
in. She didn't – didn't know where to turn. Didn't really have
anyone to turn to.

'Granddad and Ma – they'd never have understood. Mum –
Mum had to tell them lies right from the beginning, almost.
Pretend she was okay, and just couldn't visit them because
there was so much work. Or say she was in hospital for some
"woman's problem", when it was Dad – well, I guess it was a
woman's problem of sorts. Too much of a woman's problem. . .'

Joe Barnaby poured tea, then spooned decaffeinated coffee
into his cup. Daniella Ruby Gleixner sipped absently, then replaced her cup.

'Mum couldn't function without him. Oh, yes, she left him.
Then we went back. Then she left. Back we went. This went on
all through school, and into university. Mirna – Mirna turned
into daddy's little girl, even though he didn't bother to pay her
much attention at all. She was constantly looking for his approval.
It was – it was awful.

'And Mum – those mad trips she went on. Always out of the

country. It started off with flying over to Perth for an afternoon, or up to the Gold Coast. She fitted herself out with what she thought were fashionable clothes, and wormed her way into what she thought was "society". Oh, they thought they were "society" too. Lady this. Lady that. They really loved it when the journalists made an error and called them "Lady Penelope Taylor" instead of "Lady Taylor". They actually thought it made a difference, that somehow that meant they were *really* daughters of so-called nobility.' She laughed.

'I can't help sounding cynical. It's just so pathetic. And that women – women would be bothered worrying about it all! I guess their lives are so limited they'd think it worthwhile to stay with a man, or marry him, because he had a title. Well – I guess we work to change the world, and some just have to be left behind.'

Francesca Miles nodded her agreement. She preferred to think that all women, in the end, would work together for the better. But she knew, in her times of practical assessment, that what Daniella said was true. Daniella laughed ruefully, then her face grew sober again.

'Mother's life was ruined, basically. She could have been so strong – but she went to pieces. I guess the broken bones and black eyes (always well concealed – sunglasses and make up do more wonders than the cosmetic companies ever claim) didn't help. She's turned into – into someone it's difficult to care for. She turns everything into a circus. It's— '

Inspector Barnaby coughed gently. 'We talked with her some days ago. She flew from Perth to Hong Kong after the wedding – your sister's wedding. You knew that, I suppose?'

'If you're asking me did I go to Mirna's "big day" as Mum called it, then the answer's, yes.' She took more tea.

'Okay, I don't agree with marriage, weddings, the nuclear family. Well, only if the marriage lasts forever – not because it *has* to, but because the parties equally want it to; if the wedding means more than one man handing over a woman to another man; and if the family cares, rather than being exploitative and power-driven.

But Mirna's my sister. Even if the wedding gown cost three times what a woman on supporting parent's benefit gets for a year, with two children to care for. Even if the money spent on the marquee and champagne would have given us a respectable deposit on another house for a refuge at Double Bay. Even if the payment they made to Sherree Dempster to sing "I should be so lucky" could have made inroads into the infant mortality rate in Alice Springs – amazing what running water and sanitation can do!'

She took a deep breath, then said, 'Yes. I went, and I wished her luck. And I gave her my love. She deserves a happy life.'

Francesca Miles could almost see the thought going through her mind: 'But is Charles Tyson the one to give it to her?'

Daniella Ruby Gleixner crunched on a cracker, and savoured the cheese. Suddenly, a woman of about twenty-two appeared at the door. Daniella leapt up. 'Peg, what is it? Perhaps I should— ' She turned to Joe Barnaby and Francesca Miles. 'Excuse me for a moment, will you? Business.' She went out, almost pushing the other ahead of her. They heard her voice, anxious as she went.

Francesca and Joe had hardly any time to speak, before the voice returned, carrying Daniella Ruby Gleixner in its wake. Sitting down, as if there had been no interruption she went on.

'Well, like Mum, Tomas couldn't take it. Dad pushed him aside. He turned into a drunken bum. Took up shooting. Off to the gun club day and night. How he got a licence, I don't know. Shows what a hopeless licensing system there is: a drunk let loose with a gun. And he had more than one.'

She noticed the interest on Inspector Barnaby's face. 'Oh, Dad did too. It was probably his own gun that killed him. I don't know that Tomas would have the courage, anyway. He was always scared of Dad. Always. As a little boy, and as a grown man. Dad just had to look his way, and he'd quiver.

Dad's gun – no licence for him, of course. Didn't want to do it the "right" way. Not anything. Even the most obvious, easy, legal way was not for him, not for anything. If it could be done illegally, Danil Gleixner was into it. Didn't seem to want to comply with the law. Even if he didn't have to be illegal, he'd be it. Seemed to give him some sort of satisfaction – getting away with something, I guess. His life was planned around the idea of something for nothing, and he hated to pay if he didn't have to, or to regularise anything if he could avoid it.'

'When did Tomas take up shooting,' asked Barnaby. He didn't discount Daniella's assessment of her brother, but it was the first real lead on guns and the ability to use one. He couldn't let it pass.

Daniella glanced toward him, cheese and biscuit poised. 'Oh, from when he was quite young – sixteen, I think. I don't know if he joined the gun club then, but I know he went out with friends, shooting kangaroos and rabbits. Anything that moved. Horrible.'

She shuddered.

'He was almost obsessive. Then he got his girlfriends involved. That one – Jancey. Jancey Peters. She often went with him, I think. They were inseparable for a while, and I thought – well, I thought she might settle him down. Stupid me. Should have known better, what with my work in the refuge movement. We're always thinking we're going to put some man right; be his saviour; built-in social-work ethic, all of us. Well – some escape it, but not many.

'She didn't save him. And he killed her.'

Barnaby's head shot up in surprise: 'You – you mean. . .' His voice trailed off. She looked at them both, attuned to their misunderstanding.

'Oh, nothing dramatic. Happens everyday. He was drunk. Ran them into a tree. He got away without any injuries – maybe a cut to the head. One or two stitches. She was in the front passenger seat. She was trapped for hours until they got her out with acetylene torches. And it was too late. She died on the way to hospital. Tomas – Tomas got off with a bond.'

IX

In which Rosa Gleixner
Writes Herself Off

*The unfortunate part of most love affairs is that the men
are only really keen at the beginning, and the women
get extraordinarily keen just before the end.*

'THE MOTHER'S DEAD. Died six months after
the husband.' Joe Barnaby pointed at a report that lay on his
desk.

'The younger girl was fourteen at the time of her father's
death, and was sent off to live with an aunt. Susanne Robards
and the brother, Robert, were at university. Susanne graduated
just after her mother died. She worked as a pharmacist for three
years, then went overseas. She'd be about thirty now. There's no
record of her coming back to Australia, but— '

'And what about Robert?' Francesca asked, her mind half on
the despair and longing that must have led to the death of Jennifer Robards so soon after that of her husband, Tom. Danil
Gleixner had not one body, but two, on his hands, she thought.
Possibly their children had felt the same way.

'Robert's been located. He's living in Brisbane. Transferred
from Sydney University at the end of the year, and did engineer-
ing at Brisbane Institute of Technology. Been there ever since.

'Wife. Three children. In partnership with another engineer
and an architect. Oh, nothing like Eixn Enterprises. Far more
modest. But apparently doing well.'

He held up a manila folder. 'This's the report from Detective

Rubens, Queensland CIB. Had him check out Robert Robards' whereabouts on the day Danil Gleixner died. Seems it's watertight: arrived at the office, as usual, at 8.05 a.m. His secretary arrived at 8.30 and he was at his desk. She seems reliable— '

He paused, then said, 'With secretaries you never know, of course. They can be too reliable – in favour of the boss.'

'Mmm,' said Francesca Miles. 'Think of Rose Wood and the great Nixon debacle: there's a screeching sound of silence for seventeen and a half minutes on a tape; obvious it's been wiped or worse – and what does she say? Sticks up for the boss. Says it's her fault: kept her foot on the pedal of the playback machine too long when transcribing. Ridiculous. Unless the woman's a contortionist or something. Just impossible – though nothing's impossible for the boss, sometimes. Protect him at all times.'

'Yep,' Barnaby replied.

'But here, there are just too many people involved for them all to be covering up for him. Had a meeting at 9.30 a.m. with his partners. Meeting went until 11.00, and there was a secretary present to keep the minutes – someone else's secretary, not his. So – not the extreme need for loyalty there.'

Inspector Barnaby tapped with his pen on the desk. Francesca Miles' eyes ran down the open pages of the report. Barnaby was right. Robert Robards was no go.

'Perfect alibi should always be suspect,' she said, looking up at Barnaby. 'But – unless he's in it with someone else, he's out of the running.'

'Thinking of someone else,' Barnaby said slowly. 'What about the telephone call?'

'Yes, was he at the meeting the whole time – no breaks around 10.30 a.m. for instance?' Their eyes met. Was the maid's story about the telephone call genuine, a deliberate ruse to make it appear, in case anyone checked up or could check up, that the false phone call was real. Robert Robards telephoning his sister, Susanne Grace Robards, who was moonlighting as a maid in the Skye Apartments, deliberately to get back at Danil Gleixner, whom they believed had killed their father? Come back into Australia, somehow evading immigration checks at the airport – maybe got a passport in a married name, in the nationality of her husband. Working at Skye Apartments, taking time off from her profession as pharmacist, waiting for the opportunity to end Danil Gleixner's life, just as he had shortened Tom Robards' some eight years before?

'Where is the maid? Been located yet?' asked Francesca. Joe Barnaby shook his head.

'Disappeared. No one knows where or how. Took off soon after she was questioned by Constable Crawshaw. Shows either guilt or fear of being wrongly accused. Never know with people. Some think that just because they're on the spot, suspicion automatically falls on them. And for her, it's made worse, if she's not involved, by the telephone call. If she's not guilty, she'd be afraid it raises questions in our minds – as indeed it does. If she is guilty, she'd know the phone call ruse wouldn't last for long, and would have planned to make off pretty quickly after discovery of the body, anyway. The telephone call gives her an alibi, a reason for not cleaning the apartment and discovering the body. It holds us off for long enough to enable her to get away, resume some other identity – wife of some respectable businessman, probably. And no one the wiser.'

'And the notion that if she's married, she'd not have been able to moonlight as a maid without her husband's knowing has no currency,' said Francesca Miles.

'Happens all the time. Full-time housewives work as full-time or part-time prostitutes on the side, without their husbands having a clue. Get home at an appropriate hour to meet the kids from school, have dinner on the table when he's back from the office, or the factory. Wouldn't be a problem for Susanne Grace to get away with being a maid at the hours worked at Skye Apartments. Husband need never know. Children – if she has them – none the wiser.'

'Only photographs they have of her are from university days,' said Barnaby. 'Crawshaw says it's possible – but it's difficult trying to compare a face with a photograph eight years old or more.'

'It'd take a good copper to identify anyone clearly under those conditions,' said Francesca.

'Comparing a university student of eight years ago with a Skye Apartments maid'd be more difficult than most, too, I'd say: university student bedraggled; maid dressed immaculately. Hair everywhere for the student; carefully styled for the maid.'

She sighed. 'Well, what about the younger daughter... Margaret, wasn't it?'

'Got in with a bad crowd,' said Inspector Barnaby. 'Started running around with a weird lot at school, then it got worse at university. Happens to women these days.' He laughed at Francesca's expression.

'Just teasing, but you know what I mean. The aunt says she had to disown her in the end. Began bringing all sorts of weirdos home. The neighbours didn't like it. Took exception to hairy legs, apparently. At least, that's what the aunt said. She told her to leave, and to come back only when she was prepared to live a respectable life. Aunt lives at Strathfield, where I guess that means three meals a day, hot dinner at night, church on Sunday and only one late night a week. And then home by midnight.'

'So, and what's wrong with Strathfield?' laughed Francesca. '*I've* got an aunt who lives there, and she marches on International Women's Day.'

'Then she'd better look out,' rejoined Joe Barnaby. 'And better make sure she's not neighbours with Margaret Robards' Aunt Jessica, or she'll be ridden out of there on a rail.'

'WIFE STAGES SIT IN', blared the headlines. 'SUNNY HOLED UP IN SKYE', they roared. 'ROSA AND LIZ SLOG IT OUT', they clamoured.

'So, it's still going,' said Francesca Miles, looking at the array of papers spread out by Inspector Barnaby across his desk. 'Will they never stop?'

'What, the papers or Liz 'n Rosa,' asked Joe Barnaby, raising an eyebrow quizzically. 'You know, if I were Elizabeth Prince, I'd stage a sit in at the Rose Bay mansion. After all, if Rosa Gleixner's busy at the Skye penthouse, the house must be empty. Well, bar the maid and the butler and whatever other appurtenances there are.'

The 'Rosa versus Liz' saga appeared to have reached a stalemate. Rosa Gleixner had filed and served an action claiming the apartment, yacht, Monets, Manets, a Jackson Pollock, and the horses as hers, as part of Eixn Enterprises. Rumour had it she was also contemplating action claiming several expensive items of jewellery Elizabeth Prince claimed as her own, together with a number of furs and, possibly, a waterfront block: this was dependent upon title searches being undertaken. Several law clerks had been despatched at once to the Titles Office.

Shortly after the first shots were fired in what threatened to be a long-drawn-out battle, a cross-claim had been lodged on behalf of 'the mistress' (or, as the recently passed *De Facto Relationships Act* termed it, 'the de facto'), not only asserting proprietorial rights in the assets the subject of Rosa's writ, but declaiming as to a share in Eixn Enterprises – as well as the diamonds.

Maurice Burton and Simon Rees appeared daily in the *Sydney Morning Herald* and *Telegraph Mirror*, and nightly on the television news, standing solemnly outside the Supreme Court in Philip Street, or walking sternly alongside the willowy Ms Prince, steadfastly ignoring the cameras (or pretending to). They even made the *Age* some days, and the *Weekend Australian* carried a large spread on page three, then a feature article on Simon Rees' career at the Bar in the *Weekend Magazine*. Maurice Burton was (understandably, considering) upset at this added attention directed at Simon. He thenceforth managed, by nimbleness mixed with dexterity, always to be on the camera-side of the pavement as he and the other two perambulated from chambers to court. The camera operators shouted at him, sometimes, to get out of the way. They preferred to angle their lenses at Elizabeth Prince – top, bottom, sides; rear-view, front-on take; zoom from feet to face, lingering on the legs and hair. Maurice was, however, unrepentant. At least, he thought, I'm getting more coverage than Grant Webster.

Grant Webster had briefed Augustus Jones, QC, who appeared together with a senior-junior, Peter Summerhayes, and a junior-junior, Neroli Hawkins. (A Queen's Counsel could not, according to the rules of the Bar, appear alone. He – it was mostly he, although three women had been anointed Queen's Counsel in the last intake – had to be assisted by a junior barrister. In the matter of *Gleixner v. Prince*, no less than two juniors were appropriate, said Grant Webster to his employer, Rosa Gleixner. By which ruse he hoped, in the future, to 'up' his employ to that of solicitor-on-retainer to Eixn Enterprises, rather than merely to Rosa.) Cedric Augustus Jones commanded a deal of the television cameras' time, and he was always ready to conduct a 'de-briefing' session in his chambers. Discreetly, of course, so as not to upset the Bar Council: it was not that they had any intention of chastising him, or drawing a black mark against his name; no, not Augustus Jones, QC. Rather, it was that if a junior barrister – even a senior-junior – conducted himself (or even more herself) in this way, the Ethics Committee of the Bar would be obligated to hold a hearing as to the inappropriate conduct of the junior bar. A bad conduct mark would accrue – even a fine could be levied. How could the Council do its job properly, keeping the juniors in check, if Queen's Counsel blatantly flouted the rules. This would make obvious the two-standard nature of their operation: one rule for all, but in reality one for the junior Bar, none for those who had 'made it' to the lofty heights reached by those accepting a commission from the queen.

With Cedric Augustus Jones, QC as counsel, Grant Webster was unlikely to get any coverage at all, smiled Maurice Burton with some satisfaction. Oh, sometimes he'd had his sleeve pictured on the evening news, if he managed to get it into the frame which was filled, mainly, by Augustus Jones: Augustus Jones walking to and from court; Augustus Jones striding up the steps; Augustus Jones leaning casually against the base of Queen Victoria, in the square between the Supreme Court and Hyde Park. And even if his arm got near the cameras, it was usually covered by Augustus Jones' ample frame. Why, on one occasion Augustus Jones, QC had forgotten himself sufficiently to lounge casually on the ledge surrounding the Archibald Fountain near Macquarie Street. Grant Webster had thought this was his chance to star. But Cedric Augustus Jones, QC had beaten him even then, filling all available space, posterior spreading from edge to edge; thick, grey-black striped thigh pushing towards the lenses; ample biceps folded over ample chest, or flung out, frequently, to emphasise a point. The points were not, of course, made for the benefit of cameras and television viewers. Oh, no. It was quite by chance that the camera operators had found the great QC in the gardens, solemnly in conference with client and solicitor. The declaiming was not for public consumption. Well, so said Cedric Augustus Jones the following day, when he met Flinders, QC (head of the Ethics Committee) in the corridor, where they jointly deplored the invasive tactics of the modern-day media: 'No privacy, no privacy at all,' thundered

Augustus Jones, QC. 'Why, a man can't have a private conference in the outdoors any more; think they own the world, these
media moguls do,' roared Flinders, QC complicitly. They were
joined by Robalds, QC, Chairman of the Bar Council. His voice
added even more resonance to the debate; Meldromeath Chambers throbbed to the sound of counsel for the queen congratulating
counsel for the queen on his superb television performance
(although not in so many words). And they silently congratulated
each other for the virtuoso corridor performance, distancing
themselves (by their 'not in so many words') from any suggestion that Bar ethics had been breached by one-of-their-own.

'Well, I guess that proves Daniella Ruby spot-on accurate on
one thing at least,' said Inspector Barnaby, as the story raged
around them, taking over from the drama of the suicide-murder
question, the mystery of the 'locked door' to the gymnasium at
Skye Apartments, and the 'death-in-the-bath' as Tomas Gleixner's demise had come to be known by the press. 'She said Rosa
turns everything into a circus. She's right.'

'Yes,' agreed Francesca Miles. 'It sure as hell ain't pretty. And
particularly when we still don't know how Gleixner's divided
up the empire, anyway. Got any further on that one, Joe?'

'On to his solicitors Merthers, Dixon, Sandridge and Sampson,'
said Inspector Barnaby, lifting another file. 'How about an
appointment this afternoon at 2.30 p.m., Fran?'

Later, they walked back to Police Headquarters across Hyde
Park. 'Well, Daniella's got most of it, as just about everyone
predicted. But there's still enough left for Rosa Gleixner and
Elizabeth Prince to fight about until domesday,' said Joe, resort-
ing as he always did, in times of stress, to cliché.

'If it was suicide, not murder, one can only ask why,' rejoined
Francesca Miles. 'If he was worried about his financial position,
all I can say is I wish I had just that much to be worried about.'

'I guess when you're up there, you lose all sense of propor-
tion,' said Joe Barnaby, kicking at a stone with his shoe. He
noticed there was no reflecting shine; did this mean yet another

pair of shoes to be bought out of a salary that seemed just too little for a family of four, and one on the way. Oh! for the troubles of Danil Gleixner and Eixn Enterprises. *If* he *had* thought he – the corporation – was in trouble.

'Tomas was right. Left him out altogether, and the allowance stopped at Danil Gleixner's death. If Tom Eixn had lived, he'd've been dependent on his mother, or his sister, for support. For the rest of his life.'

'Or his own hands and head,' said Inspector Barnaby, sounding fierce.

'Should have pulled himself together. Hundreds – thousands of kids around the country start off much worse than him. Okay, he had a father who appears to have been more interested in business than family involvement. Who played favourites. Who bashed the kids' mother. Played around. But at least they never went hungry. Had all they wanted financially. Money and a few creature comforts can make a lot of life bearable.'

'Do you think that the lack of attention paid to him by his father eventually got to him, Joe?' mused Francesca:

'Of course it'd be a rare man who'd kill the proverbial goose that laid the golden eggs, particularly when the laying'd stop at the death. But sometimes emotions do intrude into money matters, or gain such importance they overwhelm reason. Maybe Tomas Gleixner finally allowed frustration and envy at his father's success, a success that virtually ignored him, the only son, and let fly. He's the only one so far of the lot of 'em whom we've heard with any ability to use guns, have guns at the ready. And from what Daniella says, it was more than just learning to shoot. He had pretty regular trips to the firing range. Even if a lot of it was to show off to Jancey Peters and her friends, it sounds as if he was proficient at it.'

Joe Barnaby aimed a kick at another stone, sending it shooting over towards the circular Pond of Remembrance. 'Well, I guess it's possible. Could have done it, then wallowed in remorse, deliberately drinking himself into a stupor while soaking in the bath. You'd have to know that's risky – comes into the same category as getting drunk in bed, and lighting up a cigarette. A drunk with a match is likely to end up incinerated. A drunk in a bath with a bottle could easily end up drowned. Akin to suicide. Or maybe deliberate on his part.

'But I don't know that it'd be in character – the killing, I mean. Seemed a pretty directionless type.'

'Mmm. And not a great one for making decisions, taking charge of his own life, as they say,' said Francesca.

'You can hardly think of more "direction" or taking control – in a manner of speaking – than taking a gun and shooting someone. Particularly your father. And particularly where he's so intimidating.'

'Well, we're back to accident or— '

'And if it's the "or", what's the motive?'

'Must have heard something, seen something, knew something,' said Inspector Barnaby.

'D'you reckon he could have been hanging about, saw someone go in or come out, someone who wasn't supposed to be at Skye Apartments that day? Someone who shouldn't have been there at all?'

'You mean Rosa?'

'Well – or Daniella, I guess. Or Charles Tyson: maybe he thought Mirna'd get something, even though he knew (or strongly suspected) she'd not get a major part of the proceeds. His business affairs are in a bad way. Even with Parkson Ventura's form, take more than the winnings on the horse to get him out of it.'

'D'you mean with the co-operation of Mirna, having her stand by him with an alibi at the Intercontinental. Or d'you reckon he snuck out without her knowing?'

Francesca grimaced. 'I might think he's a bit of a pain, but she's married to him. Can't see that she wouldn't miss him for the hour that it'd take to get out to Double Bay and back, with a swift despatch of Danil Gleixner in between trips. In future years maybe, maybe months or weeks, even. But not on their honeymoon.'

They crossed Liverpool Street, Joe Barnaby heading for a newspaper stand which he knew sold Mars Bars. 'IT'S KISS AND MAKE UP' proclaimed the poster advertising the early afternoon edition of the *Telegraph Mirror*. Barnaby handed over two dollars for the chocolate bar and a copy of the newspaper. 'WIDOW VERSUS WIDOW – OUT OF COURT SETTLEMENT' ran the title of the lead story.

Looking over his shoulder Francesca Miles read:

Grant Webster said today that his client, Rosa Gleixner, widow of the late Danil Gleixner of Eixn Enterprises had settled out of court her claims against Ms Elizabeth Prince, with whom Mr Gleixner had been living for some years prior to his untimely death.

Danil Gleixner was found shot in the gymnasium of the penthouse apartment he shared with Ms Prince, 33, educated at Mauriston School in Edgecliffe and Sydney University. Rosa ('Sunny') Gleixner, his wife of some 30 years, took out an injunction to recover property which she said belonged to Eixn Enterprises and was wrongly in the possession of Ms Prince. Up until today, Ms Prince was contesting Mrs Gleixner's claims.

The terms of the settlement are confidential, but sources close to the parties said they understood Mrs Gleixner has retained ownership of the Skye Apartments penthouse and the art collection, and Ms Prince has relinquished any claims she might have had in Eixn Enterprises. Ms Prince, it is understood, retains ownership of a yacht, and any other assets of the partnership she established together with Mr Gleixner. *Telegraph Mirror* enquiries have not yet uncovered what any such assets are.

The obligatory pictures appeared of Rosa Gleixner, Grant Webster again by her side (he had managed to ensure Augustus Jones, QC was nowhere about when the cameras appeared), and of Elizabeth Prince, flanked by Maurice Burton and Francis Morrish.

'So, it's all over,' said Joe Barnaby. 'At least, this round seems to be settled.'

'Yes, but who got the jewellery and furs?' laughed Francesca Miles. And, what about the diamonds? 'Sloppy bit of reporting, or was it that the "source close to the parties" let the journo down?'

They had crossed back, walking up to Oxford Square. 'Maybe we should drop in unannounced on the widow – the legal widow, that is. Ask her where she was at the time of Tomas' death,' said Barnaby. He led the way to the basement carpark.

The long, sweeping driveway up to Skye Apartments was deserted. The television cameras and journalists had left, their copy rung through or taped, the anticlimax to the 'WIVES SLUG IT OUT' story already processed for the nightly news, the morning newspapers, news updates on the drive-time and breakfast programmes. Joe Barnaby swung into a parking spot not far from the main entrance.

'She still be here, or back at Rose Bay?' asked Francesca Miles. Would Rosa Gleixner, having vanquished her one-time rival, remain at Skye, luxuriating in her victory. Or would she, once having achieved her object of banishing Elizabeth Prince from the penthouse, return to the *real* matrimonial home?

'Worth a try,' said Joe, pressing a buzzer at random, though taking care to avoid that assigned to the penthouse, so as not to forewarn anyone who might be there.

Despite the formidable look of the building, security was clearly not as it had been intended: the front door clicked, and Joe grabbed it, pulling it open; no voice sounded through the intercom system to enquire as to his identity or what he wanted.

'No need to alert Rosa that we're on our way up.' Joe Barnaby selected a floor several below penthouse level. Francesca gave him a rueful look: trying to prove he was just as fit as she, or even more so, was he? Sometimes, caution in the line of duty led to an expenditure of energy that might not be worth it, she thought. The elevator rose silently.

Climbing the broad, thickly carpeted stairs (both puffing slightly, but discreetly), they rounded the corner and saw before them the door to the Gleixner penthouse. Raising his eyebrows slightly, Joe Barnaby noticed it was ajar. Looking at Francesca, he knocked gently, a knock that might have been difficult for anyone not standing immediately behind the door to hear. He pushed. The door swung open.

Their footsteps silent on the plush pile, Francesca Miles and Inspector Barnaby advanced into the living room. The shades were drawn, thin slats of light striping the floor and lounges. Francesca's hand shot out, grabbing at Joe's arm. 'Sssh. It's Rosa. She's asleep.'

Rosa Gleixner sat in a low leather chair near a glass-topped, brass coffee table. A bottle stood beside her. She might have been snoring, but there was no sound. It was then that Francesca knew that it was not sleep. And it was not Rosa. Rather, it was death, and Rosa's body.

On the floor below her left hand lay a glass – champagne. (The thought, seeming inconsequential, passed through Francesca's mind as she took in the details.) Anchored by the bottle – Pol Roger – a creamy sheet of paper. It carried crease marks as if Rosa had folded it, then changed her mind.

Carefully, so as not to destroy any fingerprints, Inspector Barnaby picked it up, hand covered by handkerchief. 'Danil,' he read, his eyes skimming the page:

> *I can't live without you. I can only say I'm sorry. You've been everything to me. Without you, I'm nothing. There is no other way, no other life. I love you always.*

It was signed, in large, sprawling hand that was unmistakeably that of the woman whose body now sprawled in the chair, quickly cooling: 'Rosa, your only love.'

X

In which Francesca Miles Deduces Correctly

Men always think they are right about everything.
Never let a man know too much about you. Nor
should you let him know exactly what you think.

'SO – IT'S ALL over, then.' Francesca Miles was speaking, leaning back against the hard struts of a chair in Inspector Barnaby's office. 'It was Rosa – Rosa Gleixner, the wronged wife, all along.'

'That's it, Fran.' Barnaby sighed, closing the folder in front of him.

'It was champagne – and rohypnol – in the glass. Deadly when you drink too much, together. Latest thing in the Cross – and the kids are dying of it, like you never saw before. O'D-ing on heroin's nothing on this. At least with heroin, you know you're playing around with something deadly. But rohypnol? Kids think it's harmless because it's on a medical prescription. Think they can play around with it, because their mums can get it legally. And there are doctors up the Cross who don't care who they prescribe it to: minors, kids as young as ten, kids who're obviously spending their money on anything but food and a decent bed...'

His voice trailed off. Then he looked up, and began again.

'Haven't traced the source. But she could have got it from anywhere. There're doctors in Double Bay and Kings Cross who hand out prescriptions for drugs without any questions, as if they're filling orders for take-away hamburgers 'n chips. No questions asked.

Rosa'd have no problems. There was valium, serapax, mogadon, you name it, in the bathroom cabinet at Rose Bay. All on prescription.'

'But – but what about Danil? The locked door?' asked Francesca, her mind working back over the (now) string of deaths.

'Well, Fran, it wasn't locked, as you know. Not even shut properly,' said Inspector Barnaby.

'And Rosa – Rosa was as strong as an ox. Worked with Danil in the business when they were first established. Lugged engines and batteries and exhaust pipes on car jobs, got down with him on the wharves, unloading. Not beyond her to heave a tea chest or two. Or four. Shot him in the gym, then dragged him up against the door somehow, wedging him in so that he fell against it when she went.'

He tapped his fingers on the desk.

'You'll be interested in the phone call – it was genuine. Found a portable telephone back at Rose Bay, hidden in a bag Rosa brought back from Hong Kong.'

'What – you mean— ' Francesca's eyes widened.

'Yep,' said Joe Barnaby. 'Checked it out with the Duchess Aziza, Alyssia and Suzy Williams.' He drew out a sheet from the manila folder, running his finger down the margin, then looked up.

'We went back over it with them. They came off the plane together, then on the concourse going down toward customs and immigration Rosa stopped off at the first-class lounge to go to the powder room. Hadn't mentioned it the first time around. Didn't think it was important. Didn't understand we wanted every move, but *every* move.'

'And?' asked Francesca, guessing what was coming.

'She was only apart from them for a few minutes. They kept walking slowly towards the front, and she came after them. She'd done it by then, of course.'

'The telephone call,' said Francesca Miles, nodding. Barnaby nodded, too.

'Yes. The ladies powder room backs on to the Gate 11 tarmac. The wall of the cubicle at the end's all frosted glass.

And you can lower the top half. That's where she made the call to the maid. It was foolproof. Didn't have to find a phone box. Just had to make sure she had the telephone in her bag, dial out, give the message about the accident, hang up, and walk out as if she'd just powdered her nose.'

'But – but what if there'd been someone else in there,' exploded Francesca. 'She'd have been overheard. Can't have talking-to-yourself in the loo – particularly in the first-class lounge.'

'Well, Fran, we've only heard her in full voice,' said Inspector Barnaby.

'I guess if that'd happened, if the toilets had been occupied, she'd have waited and chanced the others noticing the time she was away. But you know how it is coming off those international flights. Lose sense of time. And when you're with friends, you'd be talking, not noticing how long, so long as it wasn't hours. Or she could have talked softly. I guess we're all capable of speaking sotto voce when it's really important.'

'Has the maid turned up?' Francesca was determined to have all the ends tied up.

'No,' Barnaby said. 'We've still got Crawshaw looking into it. But it'll be scaled down, now. Whether she did have some connection with Tom Robards or the Robards' family – well, the telephone call was real enough. She's been scared off by it all, poor thing. Rosa's portable telephone confirms it all – and the handbag. The three of 'em instantly recognised it as the one Rosa Gleixner was carrying on the trip back from Hong Kong. Now, why would you be lugging around an item like that unless for some purpose, Fran? Not the sort of accessory her friends knew her to take about with her.'

'Well, what about Danil? How could she be so sure he would be at Skye, rather than already departed for the city and work?' asked Francesca. Joe Barnaby leant forward, his elbows on the desk in front of him, his forefingers poised judiciously at his chin.

'I guess that's where Tomas comes in. She phoned him the night before, late. He admitted that. Maybe she got him to delay Danil somehow. Maybe she got him to telephone the next morning, before he left. Made up some story as to why he had to wait. Then Rosa sailed in with the gun, slipping out of Rose Bay with no one the wiser.'

Inspector Barnaby paused. 'It's either that, or she telephoned him, too, from the airport. Even in the short time she was away from the others, she could have made two phone calls. The others aren't positive about the precise length of time she was in the first-class lounge. You know the sort of thing. You're talking, and not noticing much. And you keep talking, and start walking without thinking about how long you had to stand waiting.'

'So, d'you say that's why – might be why Tomas ended up the way he did? Be pretty risky to include Tomas in, in any way, wouldn't it?' Francesca's brow creased, as she thought back to the interview with Tomas Gleixner.

'How could she trust him not to cotton on to what she was up to, particularly when the news of his father's death got out? Or d'you think she was aware right from the beginning that she might have to do something about him, too?'

She looked at the file in front of Inspector Barnaby, tantalisingly out of her reach, his hand casually resting on it. 'Anything to connect Rosa with Tomas' death? No one could come up with anything before.'

Francesca Miles was determined to cover everything.

'Ah, well. That's the sort of thing you've got to get used to in policework. The answer that comes when it's too late, or almost too late,' replied Inspector Barnaby.

'The slip-up by the person who's committed the so-called perfect crime. Panics. Or thinks that by getting away with it once, she'd get away with it again. The guy who believes he's become invincible.

'Then there's the passerby who saw something but didn't know she saw it. The courier who was out on deliveries on the day, and went off on holiday the next, so he's out of earshot when the calls go over the radio for witnesses to anything. Or holed herself up in some shack to write that long-planned novel, deliberately cancelling all the newspapers and never turning on the television set for fear of being distracted.'

He drew out another sheet. 'Here it is.' He pointed at a name which appeared at the head of the page, and at the paragraphs below it: 'Sam Tree. Short for Samantha, I guess,' he said, diverting slightly.

'Doing deliveries around Neutral Bay on the day. Went to the next door neighbour's to drop off a package, and saw a car right down the end of the driveway alongside Tomas' block of apartments, where it curves around to the back. Wouldn't ordinarily have seen it. Wasn't visible from the road.'

He paused again, then went on.

'Just one of the breaks of investigative work, Fran. So much depends on chance. She couldn't raise anyone at the house where she had to deliver the packet, so went around the back. There's a break in the hedge just opposite the bend in the drive. When she was coming back she noticed the car. Number plate etched on her brain.'

'So – whose was it?' Francesca looked slightly disbelieving.

'I'd say Rosa'd never be so stupid to turn up in her own car, not if she was about to knock off her own son – or anybody, for that matter.'

'Nope, you're right. It was a Budget hire car,' said Inspector Barnaby, his eyes on the paper in front of him. 'And when you know what you're looking for, it falls into place so easily,' he went on.

'Rosa got the butler, Manny Sims, to rent it. Didn't tell him what for, naturally. Just that she needed a car for that day, and he got it, no questions asked. She was out for an hour or so.'

He sighed.

'Now that she's dead, they're co-operative. But when there were questions to be answered, played the typical discreet home help: saw nothing, heard nothing, know nothing, did nothing. "Can't help, Inspector," "Unable to assist, Constable." Proverbial brick wall.'

'But why? Why Tomas?' Francesca was still puzzling it through.

'If it wasn't the phone call, then it must have been because he saw something, or knew something. Maybe he was on his way to see his father on the day, and saw Rosa there. At least we know he said she called him from Hong Kong. Maybe she just gave something away. Maybe he sensed something was up, and when Danil died, he put two and two together. Maybe he threatened her. He was probably desperate for money with his father's death, knowing he'd be dependent on Rosa, or 'd have to go begging to his sister. With a hold over his mother, he'd be set up for life.'

'So – the letter clinches it,' said Francesca slowly. 'Rosa has a conscience after all.'

'Yep. I guess the scent of battle kept her going after she did it,' said Joe.

'So long as she was engaged in a fist-to-fist with her rival, she didn't have to think about what she'd done, about the fact that she'd never get him back, once he was dead. Oh, Elizabeth Prince didn't have him any more – but by killing him, neither did she.'

'So the settlement triggered it off, then.' Francesca Miles drew a cup of mint tea toward her as she spoke. 'Once she'd come to an agreement with Elizabeth Prince, she had time to feel alone. To know Danil Gleixner would never come back to her, not ever.'

'The letter shows what she was thinking,' said Joe Barnaby. 'Probably she'd sat around drinking after her solicitor went. Grant Webster said he left at about 1.00 p.m. We got there at 5 o'clock. Four hours of thinking and drinking. . .'

'Yes,' said Francesca slowly. 'However violent he'd been toward her, however often he'd betrayed her, that he'd dumped her for a younger woman, that she'd had to leave him in the past, that she'd built up the business with him, that it'd started from funds from her own parents – all forgotten in the pain of remorse. I've read any number of—'

She halted. Not noticing, Inspector Barnaby plunged on.

'Yep. The drunker she got, the more she realised she didn't want to live without him – couldn't live without him. Wrote the letter, rohypnol and the champagne – then it's slowly, slowly, out like a candle guttering in its own wax.'

Francesca Miles eased her way carefully into the driveway that curved in front of Skye Apartments. She had arranged to meet there, at the Gleixner penthouse. Who owned it now, she was not sure. Probably, it would pass to Daniella Gleixner. Maybe Daniella would use it for that Double Bay women's refuge she had wanted to establish, maybe it would take precedence over the Roseville venture. North Shore – eastern suburbs. Not much to choose between them, probably, when you're wanting to give comfort and succour and concrete help to women beaten by powerful men.

Mmm. She'd better warn her to make sure of the security, ensure there was no more buzzing visitors in at random, no more failure to enquire of those buzzing who they were, who they wanted: their credentials, their identity even.

Francesca thought back on the previous occasions she had

visited here. First, to inspect the gym and the body of Danil Gleixner. The 'locked door' murder – or suicide, as they had wondered then. And last time, to find the body of Rosa Gleixner – the 'open door' suicide. Or was it murder, she wondered.

She was here to find out.

She pressed the buzzer to the Gleixner penthouse. Someone seemed to be expected. The front door clicked in response. She pushed, and went in.

The front door stood open. Cautiously, her mind returning to the last occasion, Francesca Miles knocked. 'Come in.' The voice sounded from the lounge. Francesca obeyed, the balls of her feet bouncing on the thickness of the carpet.

'Like a drink?' The rich-red auburn head inclined towards her, nodding her into a chair. Francesca sat. A drink? Champagne and rohypnol, she wondered. Shaking herself metaphorically, she calmly regarded her host. 'Thanks, Elizabeth. Herbal tea, if you have it.'

They were sitting in the kitchen now, perched on stools built-in to the breakfast bar. Cups stood in front of them. Elizabeth Prince's hands lay silently in her lap. They looked at each other.

'Why are you here,' said Elizabeth Prince, her voice firm, no sign of nervousness.

'I think you know that, Elizabeth,' Francesca Miles responded. 'Or do you want me to go through it all?'

The other remained confident, challenging.

'It's your show, Francesca – I may call you Francesca?'

Francesca nodded. She lifted from her lap the parcel she held there, a parcel she had brought in from her car. 'I guess it all comes back, in the end, to the Duchess of Windsor. You can never be too thin or too rich.'

Elizabeth Prince looked at her quizzically. 'You mean. . .'

'The scales. I weighed myself when I was here the first time. Just after you – after you'd found Danil Gleixner's body. Just after you'd called the police and been carted off to hospital under sedation.'

She began to unwrap the parcel on the bench.

'I weighed in three pounds over. I knew I couldn't have put on three pounds between 7.00 a.m. when I weighed myself at home, and the time I got here, to Skye. Impossible. So it was – either your scales or mine were out, or—'

She pulled a pair of bathroom scales from the wrappings. 'I thought – I thought I'd do an experiment,' she said. 'Oh, very simple. Just compare the two sets of scales.'

She slid off the stool and walked down the passage, into the main bedroom. Silently, she sensed Elizabeth Prince following her. She set the scales firmly on the carpet in front of the mirrored wall, where she had (what seemed like months ago, now) stood, weighing herself, on that day of the death of Danil Gleixner. 'What d'you reckon, Elizabeth? Will I be over or under?'

Not waiting for an response, she stood on the scales. The needle shot up, hesitated, bounced back and forth sharply, then came to a stop. 'Aha. I'm over. Again.' Her voice sounded in mock horror.

'Maybe – maybe you could give me a hand, Elizabeth. Help me to check,' Francesca Miles said. 'Let me compare my weight on this scale and on yours.'

Elizabeth Prince hesitated for a moment, then shrugged her shoulders. 'Okay, if that's what you want,' she said, looking around the room.

'If you're looking for the scales, Elizabeth, I think you'll find they're back in the gym, where they belong.' Walking over towards the gymnasium, Elizabeth Prince straightened her back, then pushed open the door. She bent, picked up something from the floor, returned. 'Here.' She set the scales next to those on which Francesca stood. Francesca transferred her weight from one machine to the other.

'Shucks,' she exclaimed in feigned anger. 'Over again!' She stepped down, then back on to the scales Elizabeth Prince had brought from the gym. 'Well, again it's either me or the scales, yours and mine. Or,' she paused, looking steadily into the other's eyes.

'Or – it's because anyone with any sense, anyone who knows anything about scales, anyone who weighs herself regularly – knows its pointless doing so when scales are on a carpeted floor. That's right, isn't it, Elizabeth?'

Elizabeth Prince's gaze faltered momentarily. Then, she returned Francesca's look with an equal steadiness as the other.

'I guess you're right. These scales were in the workout room – the floor's marble there. If you weigh in there, you'll find you'll probably come in at correct weight on both machines.'

'It's not just probable, is it, Elizabeth? It's certain.' She sat on a firm, high chair that stood beside the bed. Elizabeth Prince sank on to the bed next to her.

'You see, it was the scales that first set me thinking. I knew from the outset something was not quite right. And the more I thought about it, the more I realised it was something as silly as weight. Worrying about my weight. Thinking about the difference between my weight that morning, and how it showed up on the scales here. Knowing, without realising it, that the scales were out of place. That bathroom scales wouldn't be in the bedroom. That they'd be in the bathroom, just as the name implies. Or in the gym - when a person's got one.'

She leaned back in the chair, her back firm against the padding.

'So, I began to wonder. Worried about it in the back of my mind. Why were the scales where no self-respecting woman (or man, for that matter – as Joe Barnaby pointed out to me at the time, without realising the importance of it) would put them. And it was only – only, really, when I thought about Rosa's letter, Rosa Gleixner's letter, that I realised why.'

Her face was calm as she went on, matched only by the calm in the face of Elizabeth Prince.

'You killed him, that day, before you left for town. You were probably doing what you and he often did, or at least did sometimes, in the mornings. He'd done his workout and showered and dressed before you. You were showering. You'd worked it all out beforehand. You had the gun ready. He came into the gym, was leaning up against the door, talking with you. You walked up to him, a towel over your arm and wrist, concealing the gun. You lifted your arms, as if to hug him around the neck. And that was when you fired.'

Elizabeth Prince was silent. Whether the silence was acquiescence, Francesca was not sure. But she knew that if she had been wrong, the other would have protested before now.

'He slid down the door, to the floor. You fitted the gun into his hand, took off the clear plastic glove you'd put on to your hand and scrabbled it into the towel that was spattered.

You walked back to the shower, washed off the blood, folded the towel into a manageable wedge, and walked out of the gym.'

'But – but the door was shut. And his body up against it.' Elizabeth Prince had broken her silence, and Francesca Miles knew she was right. 'Yes – but it shut *after* you walked out,' she said, triumphantly.

'You'd done what you often do, when using the gym. We all know that gyms are notorious for poor ventilation. Even in such luxurious surrounds as Skye Apartments, it seems. You thought so, anyway. And you used the scales as a wedge between the door jamb and the door, so it created an aperture through which the steam could escape – or a body – a *thin* body.'

Elizabeth Prince's eyes flared, then she lowered her lids.

'You slid through the door, avoiding his body that was lying up against it, then pulled out the scales from the other side.

There you were, outside the gymnasium. The door jammed al-most shut. His body wedged up against the back of it. The scales in your hands. And no way, without knowledge of the scale-wedge, of knowing that someone else had been in the gym with Danil Gleixner when he died.'

Francesca Miles swooped on, clear now that she had extracted the truth from what facts she had.

'You knew that someone might notice the scales were out of place. But you didn't think the police would have a clue. Oh, certainly they're obliged to pass weight and fitness tests to get in, but we all know how little those tests mean once a guy's got into the force. The papers are full of how the police force's overweight, out of condition, attuned to desk jobs, not leaping fences at a single bound. Who'd be likely to be a fitness buff? Worried about where Danil Gleixner or Elizabeth Prince kept their bathroom scales? No. You left them in the bedroom, thinking – as so well may have easily been the case – that no one *would* notice.'

'But – but I overlooked the possibility of a woman in the force,' said Elizabeth Prince. She clapped her hand to her mouth, realising she had given herself away. But it was too late, anyway, she knew. Francesca Miles had got to the truth without any help from her.

'Yes,' said Francesca. 'And it was the same with the letter. The letter which was to be taken for a suicide note. The letter from Rosa Gleixner to Danil.' As if in answer to a silent signal, they rose together and walked to the kitchen and the comfort of tea.

'Rosa Gleixner was the victim of criminal assault at home. She was physically beaten and abused by her husband, Danil. But she kept going back. She left with the children. They stayed away for a night. Oh, sometimes for a few days. Once, Daniella said, for a longer time. They went down the coast to get away. Went back to her parents on occasion, with some made-up story. But she always returned to Danil.

'And – sometimes before she returned – she wrote him letters. Sad letters. Despairing letters. *Danil. I can't live without you. Danil. You've been everything to me. Without you, I'm nothing. There is no other way, no other life. I love you – always.*'

Francesca pressed the button on the electric kettle to reboil it. She glanced at the other woman, whose face was still.

'And why would she say: "I'm sorry"? "I'm sorry", when he's the one who's beating her. He's the one who's bashing and abusing. He's the one engaging in emotional torture?

'Because it's how all women feel. Women who've been victimised by a husband or lover. "I can only say I'm sorry."

'Sorry for – existing. Sorry for – being me. Sorry for – opening the cornflakes packet at the wrong end. Sorry for – squeezing the toothpaste tube from the middle. For cooking steak and eggs when you wanted fish and chips. Cooking fish and chips when you wanted steak and eggs. Cooking when you didn't want cooking. Not cooking when you did want it.

'Not being "good" in bed. Being too good in bed, and obviously having learnt it from the milkman, or the newsagent down the street, or the postman. Or any man. In his imagination.

'Yes. She said it many times. "I'm sorry Danil." "I can only say I'm sorry." "I'm sorry for being me."

'And she wrote it – at least once.'

Francesca Miles drew a photocopy of the letter, signed Rosa, from her wallet. She spread it out on the bench. Elizabeth Prince looked at it.

'You found it, Elizabeth, hidden away in some box or bag of Danil's. You left it here, when you were sure Rosa was dead.'

'You – you can't— ' Elizabeth Prince's voice broke. Francesca

Miles looked at her. 'No, Elizabeth, you're probably right. *I* can't prove it. But it's likely that, if they're put on the right track, the police can. Oh, you may think you've covered everything. But just as Rosa thought no one would see the car parked over at Tomas', so you've thought no one would see through your scheme. And there are bound to be errors you've made. The rohypnol prescription, for example. If the police to were to enquire of your doctor, or some other doctor you've attended, whether you've ever asked after the qualities of rohypnol, or how easy it is to get it – surely one or other of them will remember something. . .'

'But – but why would I be in a position to get Rosa to accept a drink from me, or drink in my presence, much less take rohypnol. . .' Again, her voice faltered. Again, Francesca Miles leapt in.

'Because it was all a game wasn't it, Elizabeth. A game with serious consequences. A game – played seriously.

'The "WOMAN VERSUS WOMAN" headlines: you and Rosa worked it out together, didn't you? The media was so easily beguiled, so easily fooled. The media loved it, just as you and Rosa knew the journalists and television cameras would. You had them eating from the palms of your hands – both your hands. Yours – and Rosa's.'

The kettle boiled. She poured it over a fresh scoop of tea, waiting for it to draw.

'I think you first became acquainted with Rosa Gleixner when you realised Danil was a wife beater. And that he didn't make distinctions between a legal wife and a de facto wife. That your youth wouldn't save you from his violence. That wife beating is a habit, and he had it.

You rang her one night, or one morning, after he'd been violent. You didn't know whom to turn to. Couldn't go to your mother. You didn't want to upset her. Thought she might say, "I told you so." Oh, she was impressed with Danil Gleixner's generosity, but he was a tradesman, to her, after all. Or a jumped up labourer.

'Couldn't go to your friends. Couldn't admit you'd made a mistake. And Jancey – Jancey Peters – she was dead, wasn't she, Elizabeth. Killed by Tomas Gleixner.'

Simultaneously, she and Elizabeth Prince sipped gratefully at the steaming liquid.

'So, you talked with Rosa Gleixner. And she told you what you feared was the truth. But what you didn't want to believe, not then. That he'd keep on and on. And when he'd reduced you to a thing that lived only for him, that couldn't escape if you tried, you would truly be "his".'

As if against her will, Elizabeth Prince was nodding, seemingly mesmerised. Knowing she was close to the end, Francesca swept on.

'Gradually, you built up more than a passing acquaintanceship, you and Rosa Gleixner. At some stage, you began meeting, on the sly, as it were. Without Danil knowing. And it was at one of those meetings, or gradually over time, that you and Rosa determined to kill Danil Gleixner.

'You could have left him. But he might not have let you leave. Thought he owned you. One of his possessions. And even had he, you'd have had to fight him for any recognition of contribution to assets, just as Rosa knew she'd be in a divorce battle when he chose. And he was close to choosing, wasn't he, Elizabeth. And – although most people who bothered to think about it would have thought that was what you wanted – a divorce between Danil and Rosa, and a marriage to you, you had changed your mind. Were afraid of marriage to him, of the added hold it would give him. That once you were married, he'd know he had you tied to him, and 'd look around for someone else. Use you, as he used Rosa, for his violence and for show, until he chose to redirect his "affections". That eventually, perhaps, he'd throw you over for someone else.'

Suddenly, the sound of the telephone interrupted. Elizabeth Prince hesitated, looked at Francesca, moved toward it. She picked up the handpiece. Francesca could hear a faint voice emitting from the earpiece. Elizabeth Prince responded, 'Peg. Peg. Yes. . .'

More talking.

'No. No, I can't. . . Not just now. I'm – I'm not sure when I can get away. I'm not sure when I'll be back. Can you – can you hang on for a minute.'

She glanced toward Francesca Miles, who waved at her, mouthing something.

'Excuse me, Peg, there's someone. . .'

'It'll only take another fifteen minutes or so. Tell her you'll ring back – or you'll get a message to her, shortly,' said Francesca. She had almost reached the end. She wanted to go on.

Elizabeth Prince muttered something into the phone, then hung up. She walked back to the bench, sat on the stool, took a mouthful of tea. Francesca Miles resumed.

'You planned it together. The agreement was that you would have to shoot Danil. You knew how to use a gun. Rosa didn't. She knew where the gun was, knew where he had kept the bullets. She told you he didn't have a licence for it. That he'd threatened her with it, more than once, and she'd managed to hide it from him.

'She put in the telephone call to the maid. She called Tomas from Hong Kong just before she left and made up some reason why he had to call Danil. This was a signal to you that Rosa was on her way, and that the next morning, Sydney, time, she'd be making the hoax call to get the maid away, so she wouldn't find Danil and pinpoint the time of death. Your safety depended upon there being confusion not only about suicide versus murder, but the time of death. The longer after you'd left that it seemed he died, the safer from suspicion you were. The more likely that it was suicide, not murder, because no one would have been seen in the vicinity: at least, not you, not Rosa. And it was yourself and she that you were both mainly concerned about.

'And, of course, you were concerned about Daniella, too.'

Elizabeth Prince's head shot up. 'How— ' She caught herself; willed herself to be silent. Francesca drained her cup, poured herself another.

'It depended on risk-taking. She phoned from the airport at 10.30 a.m. You killed Danil Gleixner at about 9.30 a.m. After you'd left, anything could have happened. The maid could have decided to come early to clean up. Tomas could have come knocking, wondering if anything was up. Maybe he might have suspected there was something odd in his mother ringing him and asking him to make up some story, ringing Danil.

'But you both thought it worth the danger. Your lives were untenable with Danil alive. With him dead, you both had another chance. You were prepared to run the risk.'

Elizabeth's hands were back in her lap, her face immobile, her tea growing cold in the cup.

'And it went off okay. There seemed to be no problem. You

came back, followed the plan of walking in as if you knew nothing of what you were to find. Found the gym door jammed. Telephoned the police. Gave a statement. Got yourself sedated – and it was, by that time, necessary, not simulated – and taken off to hospital.

'Rosa staged the next scene: pushed her way into Skye. Asserted her rights over the apartment, the horses, the assets of the partnership, the furs, the jewels, the yacht, the art. As you both knew she would, she commanded the attention of the media. As you knew they would, they loved the sight of the "Gleixner women saga".

'You stayed in hospital – until she telephoned you, worried about Tomas.'

The kettle was boiling again. Francesca emptied Elizabeth's cup, scooped tea leaves into the pot. Went on.

'Tomas sensed something. He wasn't sure what he knew, but he thought he knew something.

He *did* know that he had taught you to shoot. He'd taken you to his gun club, when he'd been going out with Jancey Peters, and taking her. You and she were best friends. You did almost everything together.'

'He killed her.' The words came out in a low, sharp hiss. 'He killed her, and didn't care. He got himself drunk and smashed into a tree. Got a bond. And Jancey – Jancey was – dead.'

Elizabeth Prince looked up. 'I don't care. I don't care. Anything's worth it to have got rid of Tomas. When I killed him – when I held the drunken sot down in the bath, held his feet so his head slid under the water, so he couldn't breathe, so he'd know, even if only for an instant, a little of what Jancey felt when she died. He didn't deserve to live. And I'm glad.'

'She picked you up, didn't she, Elizabeth.' Francesca's voice went on, inexorably. She had known she was right.

'She collected you from the hospital, in the car she had rented – Manny Sims had rented. Drove you to Tomas' apartment. You both knew he'd be drunk, that you might be able to persuade him to shut up, that you maybe could pay him off, keep him quiet at least until you could plan something else.

But when you walked in, he was in the bath, soaking off a hangover. A permanent hangover. You took the chance.'

'So, what are you going to do about it?' Elizabeth's voice was dull with effort. 'In the end, I had to kill her. She was losing her nerve. And – and she was going to take action against Daniella. She intended trying to upset the will. She believed she should be in charge of Eixn Enterprises. That Daniella didn't deserve it. That she'd put up with Danil all those years, and she should get back what she'd put in.

'I – I couldn't agree. Oh, I know she contributed to the business. That her parents set Danil up. That was all true. And she did deserve a proper assessment of her contribution.

'But – but she'd turned into a hater, a pure hater. It had distorted her approach to the world. She wanted to pay Danil back for everything he'd done to her. She intended to wrest the business from Daniella, and spend, spend, spend. She wanted to ruin the business, ruin it, so that Danil, whether he was up there or down below would see all his work – and hers – going for nothing. She was a hater, Rosa. She hated and hated.

'And – she – she was trying to work out some way of shafting Danil's death back on Daniella. She was hinting – hinting that Danil had interfered with Daniella when she was a little girl, and that it had twisted Daniella's mind. That Daniella hated her father and would do anything to get back at him. She was even coming to believe it – that it wasn't me – that it wasn't us who did it – killed him. That somehow, Daniella had done it.'

'And – you didn't want Daniella to be put at risk, did you, Elizabeth?' Francesca's voice was gentle.

'No. No. I— '

'Was it when you were wanting to escape from the violence?' Francesca asked. 'You said you had only Rosa to talk to. But later on, more recently, you contacted Daniella's refuge, didn't you?'

'Yes,' said Elizabeth Prince. 'Yes. It – it was a coincidence. Once – maybe the third last time he hit me, not long before – before I – shot him – I rang the refuge. I'd got the number from a leaflet in the doctor's surgery. I telephoned. And it was Daniella. It was only when we were talking – when we were talking that she worked out who I was. She didn't tell me at first. Just gave me another number to ring if anything happened. It was her home number. We – we got to talking. Only by telephone at first. I – she came to visit me afterwards – after Danil died. She said – she said I should come to stay with her and the others until I worked out what I wanted to do.

'But now— '

Francesca Miles looked at Elizabeth Prince. She considered who was dead, who was living.

Dead:

Danil Gleixner. Wife beater. Lover beater. Rip-off merchant. Evader of industrial awards. Attempted suborner of trade unions. Exploiter of women's unpaid work. Possible/probable child sexual abuser.

Tomas Gleixner. Drunk. Waster. Blackmailer. Killer with that most deadly of modern machines, the motor car.

Rosa Gleixner – this one was more difficult. Victim of wife beating. Exploited and unrecognised for her work as wife and mother. But – she had threatened to implicate an innocent woman in two deaths in which she had played a major role. Certainly accessory, and more particularly an equal principal, though she had not pulled the trigger, she had not pulled the feet. She had threatened to waste in court battles the proceeds of Eixn Enterprises. Proceeds and assets that would better be put to good use.

Living:

Daniella Ruby (formerly Gleixner) – possible/probable incest survivor. Feminist. Women's refuge worker. Advocate of world change. Controller of Eixn Enterprises' funds, assets. Donator of Eixn Enterprises' funds, assets to the women's refuge move-ment. To changing the world.

Peg Jess (formerly Margaret Jessica Robards, Francesca Miles was sure, following the feminist pattern adopted by so many women, of abandoning the family name that represented a patriarchal past, abbreviating second names, taking them on with a new, woman-centred identity) – survivor of the business ravages of Danil Gleixner and Eixn Enterprises. Feminist. Women's refuge worker, et al.

Elizabeth Prince – that, too, was more difficult. Victim – and survivor – of woman bashing. But – unlawful killer of two men. And a woman.

Francesca Miles reflected upon the nature of killing. Its unlawfulness is dictated by laws constructed, drafted, interpreted by a legal system dominated by not-women. Neither Rosa Gleixner nor Elizabeth Prince received, nor would have received, any relevant assistance from that legal system, had they sought it. 'It's a civil matter, not a criminal matter' was the litany pronounced by police, courts, magistrates, judges receiving women's complaints of criminal assault at home. Jancey Peters, unable to escape from the alcoholic clutches of Tomas Gleixner, received no help from the system. Daniella Ruby – how many children, far from being assisted by the legal system, are locked by it, into sexual abuse, whether through custody, access, or by other more blatant or more covert means.

'You were going to ring Peg Jess, weren't you?' asked Francesca. 'The telephone's over there.' She paused.

'I expect it could be seen as unorthodox for the women's refuge movement to run on the proceeds of a defunct diamond import partnership. And the sale of a yacht and furs and jewels. But you've no better use for them, have you? Unless you reserve the yacht for excursions for the shelter-children.'

Standing up, readying herself to leave, she took out her card.

'If you're ever inclined to change your mind – withdraw your support – financial and otherwise – from the women's refuge movement – remember I'm still around. And Joe Barnaby could be persuaded to realise that the case was not closed by the death of Rosa Gleixner. That the "suicide" letter was not. That the file should be reopened.

'I'll keep in touch. Just remember – you can be too rich.'